THE MAN BY THE SEA

JACK BENTON

"The Man by the Sea"
Copyright © Jack Benton / Chris Ward 2018

The right of Jack Benton / Chris Ward to be identified as the Author of this Work has been asserted by him in accordance with the Copyright, Designs and Patents Act 1988.

All rights reserved. No part of this publication may be reproduced, stored in a retrieval system, or transmitted, in any form or by any means without the prior written permission of the Author.

This story is a work of fiction and is a product of the Author's imagination. All resemblances to actual locations or to persons living or dead are entirely coincidental.

THE MAN BY THE SEA

1

The green sedan was parked at the top of the beach, its engine running, puffs of black smoke belching from its exhaust. A score-line angry enough to have been done by a key stretched in a wavering, drunken curve from under the car's left wing mirror to just above the rear wheel rim.

From his vantage point on a low headland to the beach's south, Slim Hardy lowered the binoculars, scanned the beach until he spotted a figure by the shoreline, then raised them again. With one finger he adjusted the focus until the man eased into clarity.

Wrapped in a rain jacket over his work clothes, Ted Douglas was alone on the beach. A single line of footprints in the damp sand trailed him back to the rocky foreshore.

In hands pink from the freezing wind, Ted held a book, the cover turned outward. A silver design on black, from this distance the words were unreadable. Slim wished he could get closer without being seen, but the shingle of the foreshore and the wet expanse of rock pools offered no cover.

As grey-blue waves churned and toiled, Ted lifted a hand, and a faint cry was just audible over the wind howling around the base of the towering northern cliff.

'What are you really doing?' Slim muttered. 'There's no one else down there, is there?'

He put down the binoculars and took a digital camera from his pocket. He took one snap of the car and one of Ted. Five weeks in a row Slim had captured the same pair of photographs. He was yet to say anything to Emma Douglas, Ted's wife, because, even though she was beginning to push for results, as yet there was nothing to tell.

Sometimes he wished Ted would put the book away, pull out a fishing rod, and be done with it.

At first Slim thought Ted was reading, but the way he gestured with his free hand at the sea made it clear he was either practicing a speech or reciting verse. Why, or to whom, Slim had no idea.

He shifted on grass damp with sea spray, making himself comfortable. There was nothing much to do now but see what Ted did next, to see if today he did the same as he had on the previous four Fridays: walk back up the beach, brush the sand from his clothes and shoes, climb into his car, and head for home.

Eventually, he did.

Slim followed casually, his sense of urgency shaken out of him over the last month. As before, Ted drove the fifteen miles back to Carnwell, pulled in to his driveway, and stopped his car. With a newspaper under one arm and a briefcase under the other, he headed into the comfortable house where, through a dining room window with the curtains left open, Slim watched him kiss Emma on the cheek. As Emma headed back through a door into a kitchen and Ted sat in an armchair, Slim slipped his car into neutral, released the brake, and let it roll away down the hill. As soon as he was a safe distance away, he started the engine and drove off.

Once more, he had nothing to report to Emma. One thing was certain: there was no extramarital affair, just the strange ritual beside the sea.

Perhaps Ted, an investment banker by day, was a closet Coleridge fan, slipping secretly out of work each Friday afternoon at exactly two p.m. to lambast the wild ocean with tales of albatrosses and frozen shores.

Emma, of course, as most contented wives might after being jolted out of their comfort zone by a surprise discovery, suspected a mistress.

Slim had rent to pay, a drink habit to fuel, and a curiosity to feed.

Enjoying a large glass of red over a microwave packet-curry, he perused his notes, searching for oddities. The book, obviously, was one. The scratch on the car. That Ted had perfected a ritual. Emma had said that Ted had been taking half-day Fridays for three months, only discovered when she needed to make an urgent call to the office.

An urgent call.

He made a note to ask her, but its significance was limited when Ted's ritual had been going on for so long.

There was something else too, something obvious he couldn't quite nail down. It tickled him, just out of reach.

There were other variables he had crossed off. The ritual had lasted from thirty minutes to an hour and fifteen over the five weeks Slim had watched. Ted chose his parking spaces at random. He sometimes left the engine running, sometimes not. He varied his approach and return routes each time, but not in a way as to shake a tail.

He drove so slowly that Slim—in his youth at least—could have followed by bicycle. His leisurely drive came across as mulling time, especially for a man like Ted, who Slim had witnessed during other observations driving arrow-straight to work each day, leaving home at a time that left him not five minutes for dawdling.

Whatever the reason for Ted's strange ritual by the sea, it had left Slim floundering for answers, like a fish thrown out of the water by a stormy tide.

2

On Sunday, Slim took a drive down to Ted's beach. Unnamed on the old Ordinance Survey map of the area he had bought in a thrift store, it was a narrow cove with cliffs rising to blocky headlands on either side, cupping the Irish Sea like the squeezing hands of a giant. When the tide was high, the beach was a rocky semi-circle, but at low tide a pretty field of grey-brown sand laid itself out in front of the waves.

A handful of dog walkers and a family clambering through the rock pools were the only visitors on a cheerful October day. Slim wandered down to the shoreline—the sea today a quiet ripple, the calmest he had seen it—and by looking up at the area of the southern cliff from where he watched Ted, he gauged his charge's approximate location on the last occasion he had seen him.

Just a regular patch of sand. He was standing almost central, with a few rocks over to one side, rippled sand and more rock pools to the other. The wet sand at his feet sucked at his shoes. The water was a grey line up ahead.

He was turning to leave just as a dog walker hailed

him. A Jack Russell pranced across the sand as the man, bearded and balding and wrapped in a thick tweed windcheater, swung a length of lead around like a child's lasso.

'Looks pretty, doesn't it?'

Slim nodded. 'On a warmer day I might fancy a swim.'

The man stopped, cocking his head. Fast eyes looked Slim up and down. 'You're not from round here, are you?'

Slim gave a shrug that could have meant yes or no. 'Live in Yatton, few miles east of Carnwell. Nope, us inland folk don't make it out to the coast much.'

'I know Yatton. Decent market on Saturdays.' The man turned to look out to sea. 'If you are fool enough to get into that water, make sure to watch for the rips. They're deadly.'

He said this with a certainty that sent a trickle of fear down Slim's back.

'Oh, I'll be sure to,' Slim said. 'It's too cold anyway.'

'It's always too cold,' the man said. 'You want decent swimming, go to France.' Then, touching a hand to his brow, he added, 'I'll be seeing you.'

Slim watched the man walk away across the beach, the dog making wide circles around him as it splashed through the little pools left by the departed tide. The man, occasionally jumping across deeper puddles in the sand, continued his spinning motions with the lead as though he might sometime attempt to rope the dog in. As the dog walker passed out of earshot, Slim felt a growing sense of loneliness, like a freak wave rushing in to splash around his ankles. With the wind picking up, he headed back to his car. As he was turning out of the dirt car park onto the coast road, he noticed something lying in the undergrowth just inside the junction.

He pulled up, got out, and hauled the object up out of

the weeds. The net of brambles encircling it scraped an old wooden surface, reluctant to let go.

A sign, rotten and faded.

On the downward side Slim read:

> CRAMER COVE
> No swimming at any time
> Dangerous rip currents

Slim propped the sign up against the hedge, but it lost balance and fell to the ground, face down. After a moment's thought, he left it where it lay and returned to his car.

As he drove away, up a winding coastal road cutting between two deep hedgerows as it snaked up a steep valley, he thought about what the dog walker had said. The sign explained the few people he had seen, although without the information being clearly displayed, the rips had to be local knowledge.

With a name for the beach, though, he now had something of a lead.

3

On Monday he arranged a meeting with Emma Douglas to give her an update.

'I'm close to a breakthrough,' he said. 'I just need a few more weeks.'

Emma, an overdressed but plain woman in her early fifties, removed a pair of spectacles to rub her eyes. Few age lines and hair with barely a speck of grey suggested that a husband disappearing for a few hours once a week was what she called hardship.

'Do you know her name? I bet it's that tramp from—'

Slim raised a hand, his military gaze still strong enough to sever her words mid-sentence, though he softened it with a quick smile.

'It's better that I gather everything I can first,' he said. 'I wouldn't want to pass off assumptions as truth.'

Emma looked frustrated, but after a moment's pause she nodded. 'I understand,' she said, 'but you must realise how hard this is for me.'

'Believe me, I do,' Slim said. 'My wife ran off with a butcher.'

The Man by the Sea

And it had been picking on the wrong man with a razor blade that had got him discharged from the military and hit with a three-year suspended prison sentence. Luckily, both for his freedom and his victim's face, half a bottle of whisky had reduced his aim to that of a blindfolded man thrashing about in the dark.

'I understand,' he added. 'I need you to do something for me.'

'What?'

He handed her a small plastic object. 'He wears a wind cheater when he … when I see him. Wrap this in a small piece of cloth and slip it into an inside pocket. I know those kinds of jackets. They have multiple pockets in the inner lining. He should never notice it.'

She held the item up and turned it over. 'It's a USB drive—'

'It's designed to look that way. In case he finds it. It's a remote automated bug. Army-issue.'

'But what if he checks what's on it?'

'He won't.'

And if he did, a folder of pre-loaded pornography would see it tossed into the nearest bin if Ted had any thread of decency, leaving the tiny mic hidden behind the USB casing undetected.

'Just trust me,' Slim said, hoping he sounded authoritative. 'I'm a professional.'

Emma didn't look convinced, but she gave him a shy smile and nodded.

'I'll do it tonight,' she said.

,

4

The following Friday, Slim arrived at Cramer Cove a couple of hours before he expected Ted to show up, having wanted to find a good place to set up his recording equipment. Usually he watched for Ted from an area of grass not far from the coast path, but this time he climbed a little higher and picked a grassy ledge which still had a view of the beach but was also hidden from the view of anyone who might wander past. There, with a waterproof sheet to keep off the rain, he set up his recording equipment and sat down to wait.

Ted arrived a little after two. It had been raining off and on all day, and Slim scowled as the weather worsened, threatening to disrupt his recording as the pattering of rain on his waterproof sheet intensified. Ted, wearing the raincoat, strolled to the waters' edge and took up his usual position. Today's tide was halfway up the beach. Ted was alone; the last dog walker had gone home half an hour before he arrived.

Ted squatted down and took out the book. He rested it on his knee, then leaned forward so his hood sheltered it from the rain. Then he began to read, and a muffled voice crackled through Slim's headphones.

For the first few seconds Slim adjusted the frequency control, sure he was picking up something other than Ted's voice. The words were gibberish, but Ted's gestures matched the rise and fall in intonation, so Slim sat back in the grass to listen. Ted droned on for several minutes, paused for a while, then began over again. Slim found his attention drifting as he struggled to make any sense of the words. By the time Ted implored in English, 'Please tell me you forgive me,' Slim had been studying the gently rolling waves for some minutes, thinking about something else.

Slim sat up as Ted stuffed the book back into his coat pocket. After one last glance out to sea, Ted turned and walked back to his car, head lowered. Slim began to stuff his gear into a bag. His fingers tingled, his mind raced. Something felt wrong, as though he had intruded on an act that was private and should never be shared. As he looked up to see Ted's car pulling out of the car park, he knew he should give chase, that tonight might be the night Ted sped off into the arms of some hitherto unseen lover, but he was frozen, caught in his own riptide by the threat of what Ted's words might reveal.

5

That night, still without making any decisions on what to do about the mysterious recording, Slim dreamed of crashing waves, and grey-blue arms reaching up from the freezing depths to pull him down.

Aware his discharge was coming, Slim had salvaged what he could from the army, and in the fifteen years since, and particularly in the five since he had quit a succession of low-paid, lower-interest trucking jobs to start out as a private investigator, he had made good use of his contacts. Late the next morning, with a bowl of cornflakes in hand —spiced with a dash of whisky—he made a call to an old friend who specialised in foreign languages and translation.

While waiting for a response, he climbed back into bed and pulled his old laptop up onto his knees. The Internet, with a little probing, began to reveal answers.

Cramer Cove was unlisted among the Lancashire coast's best tourist spots for more than thirty years. According to a local legislation website, bathing was banned after the summer of 1952, when the powerful rips had claimed three lives over the course of a few weeks.

With any kind of water activity officially off-limits, the death knell had sounded for Cramer Cove as a summer hotspot, with locals and tourists alike abandoning the picaresque cove for the blander but safer sands of Carnwell and Morecombe. However, a few hardy souls had clearly braved it, as there were another four known deaths since the early 1980s, and while the circumstances surrounding each were more mysterious, all had officially been attributed to drowning accidents.

As the trail of tragedy lengthened, Slim felt reluctant to deepen his search. His one active tour during the first Gulf War in 1991 had destroyed much of his curiosity. There was a level for which the lift should be permanently disabled, and he already felt way beneath it, but he was on a different kind of payroll now, and his rent wouldn't pay itself.

He checked dates against ages. Ted Douglas was fifty-six, so in 1984 he would have been twenty-three.

And there she was.

October 25th, 1984. Joanna Bramwell, aged twenty-one, presumed drowned at Cramer Cove.

Was Ted lamenting a lost love? According to the details Slim had requested from Emma Douglas, they had met and married in 1989. By then Joanna Bramwell had already been dead five years.

Slim was glad there was no affair. It was far too ordinary, an anticlimax in many ways.

The Internet closed shop at a name and cause of death, so Slim coaxed life into his old Honda Fit on a chilly morning and drove down to the library in Carnwell to trawl through microfiched newspaper archives.

The three victims after Joanna were a teenager, a child, and an elderly lady. When Slim got to a page that should have run an article about Joanna's death, he found the page smeared as though water-damaged, the words blending into each other, unreadable.

The duty librarian claimed there was no other copy, despite Slim's protestations. His request for information on the cause of the damage was met by a shrug.

'You're looking for an article on a dead girl?' asked the librarian, a man in his thirties, who had the look of a wannabe-novelist, all roll-neck sweater, ornamental scarf, and wire-framed spectacles. 'Maybe someone doesn't want you to read it.'

'No, maybe not,' Slim said.

The young librarian actually winked, as though this were some kind of game. 'Or maybe the person you're looking to dig up would prefer to remain undisturbed.'

Slim forced a smile and what he considered the expected chuckle, but as he left the library, all he felt was frustration. Joanna Bramwell, it appeared, did indeed wish to remain undisturbed.

6

The army, for all its rigidity and rules, had taught Slim resourcefulness, and made him master of a cacophony of disguises he could assume at will. Armed with a clipboard, a blank notebook, and a pen borrowed indefinitely from the local post office, he drank his way through a few hours masquerading as a local history documentary researcher, knocking on door after door, asking questions only of those old enough who might know, running his mouth to distract those too young who wouldn't.

Nine streets and no substantial leads later, he returned, drunk and exhausted, to a missed call on his flat's landline from Kay Skelton, his translator friend from the army, who now worked as a forensic linguist.

He called back.

'It's Latin,' Kay said. 'But even more archaic than usual. The kind of Latin that not even people who speak Latin would generally know.'

Slim sensed that Kay was simplifying a complicated concept that he might fail to understand, but went on to explain that the words were a call to the dead, a lament to a lost love. Ted was begging for a recall, a resurrection, a return.

Kay had scanned the transcript online and found it a direct quote, taken from a 1935 publication entitled *Thoughts Encompassed upon the Dead*.

'Likely your mark picked the book up in a junk shop,' Kay claimed. 'It's been out of print for fifty years. What kind of man wants something like that?'

Slim had no answer, because, frankly, he didn't know.

7

Another week of pretend-researching brought Slim another lead. At the mention of Joanna's name, a smile came over the face of an old lady who introduced herself as Diane Collins, local nobody. She nodded with the kind of enthusiasm of someone who had not had a guest in a long while, then invited Slim to sit in a bright living room with windows looking out over a manicured lawn sloping down to a neat, oval pond. The only thing out of place was a bramble making its way up the wooden fence at the garden's rear. Slim, whose knowledge of gardening extended only as far as occasionally kicking aside the weeds on his building's front step, wondered if it might actually be a rose branch lacking any flowers.

'I was Joanna's form teacher,' stated the old lady, hands encircling a cup of weak tea, which she had a habit of revolving in her fingers as though bidding to ward off arthritis. 'Her death shocked everyone in the community. It was so unexpected, and she was such a lovely girl. So bright, so beautiful. I mean, there were some real terrors in that class, but Joanna, she was always so well-behaved.'

Slim listened patiently as Diane began a lengthy monologue about the merits of the long-dead girl. When he was sure she wasn't watching, he slid a hip flask from his pocket and poured a drop of whisky into his tea.

'What happened on the day she drowned?' Slim asked, when Diane began to digress into tales of her teaching days. 'Didn't she know about the rips at Cramer Cove? I mean, Joanna wasn't the first to die down there. Nor the last.'

'No one knows what really happened, but her body was found at the high tide line early in the morning by someone walking a dog. By then, of course, it was too late.'

'To save her? Well—'

'For her wedding.'

Slim sat up. 'Say again?'

'She disappeared the night before her big day. I was there, among the guests while we waited for her. Of course, everyone assumed she had jilted him.'

'Ted?'

The old woman frowned. 'Who?'

'Her fiancé? His name was—'

She shook her head, waving away Slim's suggestion with the flap of a liver-spotted hand.

'I don't recall now. I remember his face, though. Picture was in the paper. They never should have photographed a man heartbroken like that. Although, I should say, there were rumours…'

'What rumours?'

'That he knocked her off. Her family had money, his didn't.'

'But before the wedding?'

'That's why it never made sense. There are better ways to knock someone off though, aren't there?'

The Man by the Sea

The way Diane looked up and gazed at him made Slim feel like she was looking into his soul. *I never killed anyone,* Slim wanted to tell her. *I might have tried once, but I never did.*

'Was there an investigation?'

Diane shrugged. 'Of course there was, but not much of one. This was the early Eighties. In those days a lot of crimes went unsolved. We didn't have all these forensics and DNA testing and all that you see on the TV now. Questions were asked—I remember being interviewed myself—but with no evidence, what could they do? It got written off as an unfortunate accident. For some silly reason she went swimming the night before her wedding, got out of her depth, and drowned.'

'What happened to her fiancé?'

'He moved away, last I heard.'

'And the families?'

'I heard his went overseas. Hers moved south. Joanna was an only child. Her mother died young, but her father just died last year. Cancer.' Diane sighed as though this was the height of the tragedy.

'Anyone else you know of that I could talk to?'

Diane shrugged. 'There might be old friends around. I wouldn't know. But be careful. It isn't talked about.'

'Why not?'

The old lady put down her tea on a glass-topped coffee table with tropical butterflies beneath its pressed surface.

'Carnwell used to be much smaller than it is today,' she said. 'These days it's become something of a commuter town. You can walk to the shops now without seeing a single familiar face. It never used to be that way. Everyone knew everyone, and like every close-knit community, we had baggage, business we'd rather stayed secret.'

'What could be that bad?'

The old lady turned to look out of the window, and in profile Slim could see her lip was trembling.

'There are those who believe Joanna Bramwell is still with us. That … she haunts us still.'

Slim wished he'd put a stronger measure of whisky in his tea. 'I don't understand,' he said, forcing a smile he didn't feel. 'A ghost?'

'Are you mocking me, sir? I think it's perhaps time you—'

Slim stood up before she did, putting up his hands. 'I'm sorry, madam. It's just that this all sounds unusual to me.'

The woman stared out of the window and mumbled something under her breath.

'I'm sorry, I didn't catch that.'

The look in her eyes made him shiver. 'I said you wouldn't say that if you'd seen her.'

As though a battery had run to its last, Diane would say nothing more of interest. Slim nodded along as she led him back to the front door, but all he could think about was the look in Diane's eyes, and how it had made him want to look over his shoulder.

8

Slumped over a plate of reheated pizza, Slim mulled over what he ought to tell Emma.

'I think my husband is having an affair,' had begun Emma's first recorded phone call to Slim's mobile. 'Mr. Hardy, would it be possible to call me back?'

Affairs were easy to prove or disprove with a little stalking and a few photographs; they were bread and butter to private investigators, the kind of easy pickings that paid mortgages. He had already dealt with that job. Ted was in the clear, unless it was possible to have an affair with the ghost of a drowned girl.

Emma had offered to pay on information, and Slim's account was running low. But how could he explain the ritual Ted played out every Friday afternoon?

He arranged a meeting with Kay in a local café.

'It's an ancient ritual,' Kay told him. 'It calls on a wandering spirit to return to the place it calls home. Your mark is asking a spirit to return to him. I matched part of the text to the manuscript I found in an online archive, but another part has been changed. It's rough, the grammar a little uncertain. I think your mark did it himself.'

'And what does it say?'

'It asks that he be given a second chance.'

'You're sure about that?'

'Quite sure. But the tone ... the tone is off. It might be a translation error, but ... the way he says it, it's like something bad will happen if she doesn't come back.'

Kay agreed to translate the following week's ritual too, to see if there was any variation, but following that, regretfully, he said he would need something for his time.

Slim needed to say something to Emma. Expenses, both actual and possible, were beginning to mount up. First, though, he tried to pull another of his frayed old army strings, to see if he could dig up a little more background.

Ben Orland had worked in the military police, before taking up a superintendent post in London. While his tone was cold enough to remind Slim of the disgrace he had brought to his division, Ben did offer to make a call on Slim's behalf to an old friend, Carnwell's police chief.

The police chief, however, wasn't returning calls to internet-based private investigators.

Slim decided to compile what information he had so far to pass to Emma, and leave it at that. After all, he'd achieved his initial commission, and if he let himself dig too much deeper, it would be on his own time and at his own expense.

First, he swung past Cramer Cove to take a stroll, wondering if the wild headlands might inspire him.

It was Thursday, and the beach was deserted. With the windy approach road, potholed, and in places so broken up it was little more than a dirt track over stones, it was no

The Man by the Sea

surprise that Cramer Cove was unpopular. Yet at the top of the beach he found stone foundations suggesting it had enjoyed far greater popularity in bygone days.

On the plateau above the foreshore, Slim found pieces of wood lying in the weeds, traces of garish paint still visible. He closed his eyes and turned around, breathing in the scent of sea air and imagining a beach crowded with tourists, sitting on towels, eating ice-creams, playing with balls on the sand.

When he opened his eyes, something was standing by the distant water's edge.

Slim squinted, but his eyes weren't what they had once been. He patted his jacket pocket, but he had left his binoculars in the car.

The thing was still there, a jumble of greys and blacks in a human shape. Water glistened on its clothes, in the long threads of tangled hair.

As Slim watched, it melted backward into the sea and was gone.

He stared after it for a long time, dumbstruck, and as the minutes ticked by, he began to doubt whether he'd really seen anything at all. Just a shadow, perhaps, as a cloud passed over the beach. Or even something not human at all, one of the grey seals that populated this section of coast.

He tried to remember how many drinks he'd had today. There had been the usual dram in his morning coffee, a glass—or was it two?—with lunch, and perhaps one before he set out?

It might be time to consider easing back. He played roulette every time he stepped in the car, but he had spent so long suppressing the guilt and shame of his own existence that he barely noticed it anymore.

He was counting possible drinks on his fingers when he realised that the tide was not yet low. If something had really been there, tracks would be visible in the wet sand.

Slim climbed over a rusty metal barrier, hurried down the rocky foreshore and out across the sand flat. Long before he reached the water's edge he knew his search was futile. The sand was smooth, scored only by ripple lines left by the receding water.

By the time he returned to his car, he had convinced himself that the figure watching him from the shoreline was a figment of his imagination.

After all, what else could it be?

9

The following Friday, Ted repeated his ritual as usual. Slim had considered meeting Emma in the morning and then bringing her along to prove his story, but after a night filled with vicious dreams of sea demons and crashing waves, he thought better of it. Watching Ted from the same grassy ledge he had watched from over the five previous weeks, he felt strangely redundant, as though he'd run hard at a brick wall and had nowhere left to go.

Walking back down to the beach after Ted had gone, he kicked at the faded pink remains of a plastic spade and decided it was time to do some more digging.

He figured Saturday and Sunday were the days when most people would be at home, so he trolled the streets, knocking on doors and posing questions in his newly familiar guise as a fake documentary maker. Few people would give him the time of day, and by the time he'd stopped by three of Carnwell's pubs to tally up what he'd learned so far, he doubted he was in the kind of state to make much headway anyway.

He was stumbling along one last street on the northern

edge of the town when a siren gave a quick blare to announce a police car pulling in behind him.

Slim stopped and turned, leaning on a lamp post to catch his breath. A police officer rolled down a window and waved to Slim to get inside.

In his early fifties, the man had ten years on Slim but looked fit and healthy, the kind of man who ate muesli and orange juice for breakfast and went for a lunchtime run. Slim fondly remembered the days when he had seen such a man staring back at him, but it had been a couple of years since he had dropped and broken his flat's only mirror, and he never looked too hard at reflections in case the bad luck was catching.

The police officer smiled. 'What's this about then? Three calls I get today. Doubled the weekly average. Which house are you planning to burgle?'

Slim sighed. 'I guess if I had to choose, I go with that green one on Billing Street. Number Six was it? Husband at work yet two Mercs in the drive? You could tell just from the hum of the air-con that the house is a treasure trove. I mean, who has A.C. in northwest England? I'd be in there already, but I didn't fancy risking that the alarm just inside the door having a direct police link up.'

'It does indeed. Terry Easton is a local lawyer.'

'Bloodsuckers.'

'You got that right. So, I'm guessing, Mr—'

'John Hardy. Call me Slim. Everyone does.'

'Slim?'

'Don't ask. It's a long story.'

'As would be appropriate. So, I'm guessing, Mr. Hardy, that you're not really interested in local myths and legends. What are you, Scotland Yard undercover?'

'I wish. Military intelligence, discharged. Attacked a

man who wasn't actually banging my wife. Did my time, came out with a prior skill set and a drinking problem waiting to happen.'

'And now?'

'P.I. Work mostly around Manchester. Starvation brought me this far north.' He patted his stomach. 'Don't be fooled. It's only beer and water.'

As if unsure where Slim was crossing between truth and humour, the man gave a tentative smile. 'Well, Mr Hardy, my name is Arthur Davis, Carnwell's police chief, though with the size of our force I barely deserve the title. I believe you tried to contact me about a cold case. Joanna Bramwell?'

'Is this how you usually return calls?'

Arthur laughed, a baritone that made Slim's ears ring. 'I was heading home. Thought I'd keep a look out for you. Now, do you want to tell what this is about? Ben Orland is an old friend, which is the only reason I even considered speaking with you. There are cold cases, and then there's the case of Joanna Bramwell. It's one this community has always been happy to keep buried.'

'Any particular reason?'

'Why do you even want to know?'

Without asking, Arthur had driven into a drive-through MacDonalds and presented Slim with a steaming cup of black coffee.

'I take three sugars,' Arthur said, ripping open a sachet. 'You?'

Slim gave him a tired smile. 'Dram of Bells if I've got one handy,' he said. 'But I'll take it straight. Over-percolated works best.'

Arthur pulled into a free parking space and shut off the engine. In the glow of the nearest streetlight, the police chief's face was like the surface of the moon, a series of shadowed craters.

'I'll tell you straight up that you should leave this case alone,' Arthur said, sipping his coffee, staring straight ahead at the railings that separated them from a ring road roundabout. 'The Joanna Bramwell case broke one of the best policemen Carnwell ever had. Mick Temple was my first mentor. He led that case but retired straight after, aged just fifty-three. Hung himself a year later.'

Slim frowned. 'All because of a dead girl on the beach?'

'You're a military man,' Arthur said. Slim nodded. 'I guess you've seen things you don't like to talk much about. Unless you've had a drink, and then you'll talk about nothing else?'

Slim watched the lights of cars blurring along the ring road. 'An explosion,' he muttered. 'A pair of boots and a hat lying in the dust. Everything in between ... gone.'

Arthur was silent for a few seconds as if digesting this information and giving it a customary period of respect. Slim hadn't spoken of his old platoon leader in twenty years. Bill Allen hadn't disappeared completely, of course. They had found bits of him later.

'Mick always said she came back,' Arthur said. 'They found her lying high on the foreshore, as though carried there by a freak wave. You've been to Cramer Cove, I take it? She was thirty metres above the spring tide line. No way Joanna could have got there unless someone dragged her.'

'Or she crawled there herself.'

Arthur put up a hand as though to push the thought out of his mind.

'The official report stated that the two dog walkers who found her must have moved her, to keep her away from the tide, but both were local residents. They would have known the tide was going out.'

'But she was dead?'

'Quite. Coroner examination and everything. Officially, she drowned. They put her in the morgue and later they buried her.'

'And that's it? No investigation?'

'We had nothing to go on. No suggestion it was anything other than an accident. No witnesses, nothing circumstantial. It was an accident, that was all.'

Slim smiled. 'So why did you call it a cold case? That's an unsolved murder investigation, isn't it?'

Arthur drummed his fingers on the dashboard. 'You got me. It's forgotten to everyone except those few of us who remember Mick.'

'What else do you know?'

Arthur turned to face Slim. 'I've told you enough, I think. How about you tell me what you're doing out trolling Carnwell's streets in search of information?'

Slim thought about spinning the police chief a lie. After all, if he'd opened a can of worms and the police got involved, he'd likely never get paid. 'In the end he said, 'I have a client who has an obsession with Joanna. I'm trying to find out why.'

'What kind of obsession?'

'An, um, occult one.'

'Are you one of those wacko ghost hunters?'

'I wasn't until a week or two ago.'

Arthur groaned. 'Well, this would be a good place to start. You heard of Becca Lees?'

Slim frowned, searching his recent memory. The name appeared somewhere—

'Second victim,' Arthur said. 'Five years after the first. 1992. There was a third in 2000, but we'll get to that.'

'Should I be writing this down?'

In the gloom, Arthur's gesture could have been a nod or a shrug. 'I'm not talking to you right now,' he said. 'You'll discover this on your own, in the end.'

'But it would suit your purpose if the Joanna Bramwell cold case was ... warmed up a little?'

'Mick was a good friend,' Arthur said.

Slim sensed the matter was closed. 'What do you have for me?'

'Becca Lees was nine,' Arthur continued. 'Found in the pools on the beach's south side at low tide.'

'Drowned,' Slim said, remembering what he had read of the story. 'Accidental death.'

'Not a mark on her,' Arthur added. 'I was in the first car on the scene. I—' Slim heard a sound like a suppressed sob, '—I rolled her over.'

'I've heard a lot about those rip tides,' Slim said.

'It was October,' Arthur said. 'Right about this time of year. Half term week, but we'd had a storm roll in and the beach was covered in debris. Young Becca, according to her mother, had gone down to collect driftwood for a school art project.'

Slim sighed. 'I remember once doing the same. And she decided to take a quick swim, and got pulled in.'

'Her mother dropped her off on the way into Carnwell. Came back an hour later to pick her up, and it was too late.'

'You think she was murdered?'

Arthur thumped the dashboard with a ferocity that made Slim flinch.

'Goddamn it, I know she was murdered. But what

The Man by the Sea

could I do? You don't murder someone on a beach unless it's already low tide. Know why?'

Slim shook his head.

'You leave tracks. Ever tried brushing away tracks left in sand? Impossible. Yet there was one set. That's all. Down to the water's edge, then there was a small space where the tide had gone out. The girl had been dragged through the water and dumped on the rocks, left marooned when the water receded.'

'Sounds like drowning. She got too close, got sucked under, dragged across the beach.'

'So it appears. Except Becca Lees couldn't swim. She didn't even like the beach. She had no swimsuit with her. We show up, and there's a zigzag across the sand where she's picking stuff up. Then from about halfway to the low tide mark, there's a single straight line up to the water's edge, which ends with two prints in the sand, facing out to sea. What does that tell you?'

Slim let out a deep breath. 'That either a girl who didn't like water felt a sudden urge to walk right up to the shore ... or she saw something that caught her attention.'

Arthur nodded. 'Something that came out of the water.'

Slim thought of the figure he thought he'd seen by the shore. Had Becca Lees seen something similar? Something that had compelled her to leave her driftwood collecting and walk straight to the water's edge?

Something that had lured her to her death?

'There's something else,' Arthur said. 'The coroner picked it up but it wasn't enough to stop a ruling of accidental death. The muscles in the back of her shoulders and neck displayed an unnatural tightness, as though they had stiffened immediately after her death.'

'How could that happen?'

'I talked to the coroner, and I put it to the superintendent as my reasoning for extending the investigation, but there was no other evidence. What it could have proved was that Becca was trying to withstand a great pressure at the moment of her death.'

Slim nodded. He rubbed his eyes as though hoping to banish an unwelcome image from his mind. 'Someone was holding her under.'

They exchanged numbers before Arthur dropped Slim off near his place with a promise to dig out whatever he could find of the case files. There was more to tell, he said, but with a wife and dinner waiting it would have to hold over for another time.

Slim, with his brain frazzled after an exhausting day, had come to only one concrete conclusion: he needed to talk to Emma about Ted.

10

He met Emma in a forest park a couple of miles out of town. She had picked the location as one where they were least likely to be seen, where they could conduct their business with no way of it finding its way back to Ted. As he waited for her, Slim was plagued by the feeling that they were a pair of secretive lovers, and the loneliness that walked with him everywhere enjoyed the analogy rather more than he felt was appropriate. As Emma approached, walking briskly, her head lowered, Slim stuffed his hands deep into his coat pockets, lest they could in some way betray him.

Emma's expression was terse. 'It's been almost two months,' she said. 'Do you have answers for me yet?'

No formal greeting. And the analyst in Slim wanted to point out that it was seven weeks and four days.

'Mrs. Douglas, please sit down. Yes, I have some information, but I also need some.'

'Oh, right, Mr Hardy, you're on my payroll but you're still figuring things out, is that it?'

Slim was tempted to mention that he was yet to receive

a penny. Instead he said, 'It is my conclusion that your husband is not having an affair—' The relief on Emma's face was somewhat tempered by Slim's final word: '—yet.'

'What are you talking about?'

'I believe, at this point that your husband is attempting to contact a former girlfriend or lover. To what end, I'm not sure, but the obvious one comes to mind. However, I need to go over your husband's background one more time in order to fully establish what kind of relationship Ted has or wants with the person he is trying to contact.'

Slim mentally scolded himself for treating speculation as fact, but he needed to loosen her tongue.

'That bastard. I knew we should never have come back here. Everyone's screwing each other in these horrible little inbred towns.'

Slim wanted to point out that if Carnell was in the grip of a mass orgy he'd been regrettably overlooked, but instead he tried to force a look of sympathy into his eyes.

'Three years ago, you told me, wasn't it? That you came back here?'

'Two,' Emma said, correcting Slim's deliberate mistake. She took a deep breath, lining up a slew of background information that Slim hoped would contain something he needed. It was always best when a client told you before they were asked. It made the tongue, often such a suspicious beast, into a willing companion.

'He got offered a job, so he said. I was happy in Leeds. I had my part time work, friends, my clubs. I don't know why he wanted to come back. I mean, his parents are long gone and his sister lives in London—not that he ever calls her—so it's not like he has any ties here. I mean, we've been married twenty-seven years, and he's only ever driven me through it a handful of times on the way to somewhere more interesting. Okay, there was this one time we stopped for chips, but they really weren't nice, far too dry—'

'And your husband, he's in banking?'

'I've told you all this before. Investment. He spends all his time knee-deep in other people's money. I mean, it's a soulless existence, isn't it? But we can't always make money doing what we want in life, can we, Mr. Hardy?'

'That's true.'

'I mean, if we could, I'd be paid for drinking port at lunchtime.'

Slim smiled. Perhaps he had found a kindred spirit after all. Emma Douglas was ten years older than he at best, but she had looked after herself in ways that women with Christmas gym memberships and too much free time were wont to do. In the interests of closing the case, he realised that, with a drink or two in him at least, he'd do whatever was necessary if it meant keeping tongues loose.

And to hell with morals.

'And your husband's background ... he was always into finance?'

Emma snorted. 'Oh, good God, no. He tried his hand at all sorts, so I believe, after he graduated. But there's not much money in rubbish like poetry, is there?'

Slim lifted an eyebrow. 'Your husband was a poet?'

Emma waved a dismissive hand. 'Oh, he was into all that. He studied English classics. You know, Shakespeare?'

Slim allowed himself not to be offended. 'I know a few of the titles,' he said, hiding a smile.

'Yes, Ted loved that kind of thing. He was a real hippy back in the late Seventies. Tried his hand at stand-up poetry, acting, that kind of thing. He graduated in eighty-two, and worked for a while as a substitute English teacher. Doesn't really pay the bills, though, does it? It's nice when you're young to be into all that, but it's not something to do long-term. A friend got him a banking job shortly after we were married, and I think he found the income quite addictive, as one might.'

Slim gave a slow nod. He was painting as much a picture of Emma as he was of Ted. The repressed romantic, shoehorned into a life based on money, with a materialistic, trophy wife glued to his arm, pining of the old days, of poetry, freedom, and perhaps beaches and old lovers.

'Does Ted often talk much about the old days? I mean, before you were married?'

Emma shrugged. 'He used to, sometimes. I mean, I never wanted to hear about old lovers or anything like that, but he would talk about his childhood from time to time. Less as the years passed. I mean, no marriage stays as it was, does it? People don't talk like they used to. Didn't you find it that way?'

'Me?'

'You told me you were married, didn't you?'

Sometimes, painting himself as a victim made people open up, and he needed Emma to feel a certain companionship before he asked the next, difficult, questions.

'Nine years,' he said. 'We met when I was on recuperation leave after the first Gulf War. I was in barracks most of that time during our marriage. Charlotte joined me on the first couple of bases, when I was stationed in Germany. But she didn't fancy Egypt, or later Yemen. She preferred to stay back in England and "keep house", as she put it.'

Emma put a hand on his knee. 'But what she was

actually doing was taking control of your finances and taking other men into your bed?'

Had the choice of words been his, Slim, who watched far fewer daytime soaps than it was clear Emma did, would have phrased it differently, but it wasn't altogether untrue.

'That's about the whole of it,' he said. 'She was happy enough until a minor wound hunting pirates in the Persian Gulf got me transferred to military intelligence back in the U.K. Then I could go home at weekends. She lasted a month before she ran.'

'With the butcher?'

Slim smiled. 'Did I tell you about that? Yes, with the butcher. Mr. Staples. I never learned his first name. I didn't find out until later. She'd been flirting with a colleague who announced he was moving to Sheffield. I put two and two together and got screwed.'

'Poor you.' Emma patted his knee, then gave it a slight squeeze. Slim tried to ignore it.

'It is what it is. I don't miss the military one bit. Life is so much more interesting as a P.I., surviving from payday to payday.'

'Well, I'm glad,' Emma said, missing Slim's heavy dose of sarcasm.

'It got worse,' Slim continued, going for the killer blow that would seal them as pity buddies forever. 'She pulled a few legal strings while I was in service. She filed for divorce and I found out the house I was paying for had been changed solely into her name. She claimed it as a pre-existing property she had owned before our marriage. She'd had someone tweak a few dates on legal documents and I lost everything. Oh, and she was pregnant, which got her additional leniency. This after aborting our first child while I was on active duty, because she didn't want the baby growing up without a father.'

'The second baby was yours?'

Slim laughed. 'Hell, no. I hadn't been near her in years. I presume it belonged to the butcher, like the rest of my life then did.'

'Oh, that's awful. Emma was stroking his thigh, but Slim, with his hands still stuffed deep into his pockets, ignored it. Instead, he shrugged. 'One of those things,' he said.

'It must have been heartbreaking.'

Slim closed his eyes a moment, remembering a pair of boots sitting on the sand. 'I've seen worse,' he said.

Emma was silent for a moment, frowning as she stared at the path, hand still working up and down Slim's thigh as though trying to warm it against the cold.

'Can I ask you a personal question?' Slim said.

'How personal?'

'Would this be Ted's first affair?'

Emma withdrew her hand and appeared taken aback. 'Um, well, I believe so. I mean, I'm not sure, but he's always been a good husband.'

'And yourself?'

'What?'

'I'm sorry to ask you this, Mrs. Douglas, but have you?'

Emma pulled away from him. The vacant space between them on the bench stared at Slim like a wide-eyed child.

'What's that got to do with anything?' Emma stood up and backed away. 'Look, Mr. Hardy, I think it might be time I terminated our contract. You've given me nothing of any value and now you're asking me questions like that. I'm not some lonely wife you can just—'

'Did Ted ever show any interest in the occult?' Slim interjected.

Emma stared at him, open-mouthed, then shook her head. 'I never should have hired you,' she snapped. 'I'll find out what's going on by myself.'

Without another word, she stalked away, leaving Slim sitting alone on the bench, his fingers caressing the warm place her hand had left on his thigh.

11

With no better ideas, Slim headed for the library and checked out a Shakespeare anthology. Then, an hour later, he was back at the desk beneath the condescending gaze of the wannabe-writer clerk to return the book—which had been as useful as reading French—and in its place rent the library's DVD film copies.

By Thursday night, after a two-day television binge, he had watched all of the films he had heard of, and a couple he hadn't. Even seeing the drama played out, a lot of it had made little sense, but if Ted Douglas had spent his formative years engrossed with the likes of Hamlet and Macbeth, it was easy to see where an interest in the occult might have come from.

Drunk on cheap red wine, Slim dozed through the closing scenes of Romeo and Juliet, waking up when his phone rang to find both lovers dead and the credits rolling.

He wasn't quick enough out of the chair to pick up the call, and the caller left no message. Checking the number, he found it unrecognised, and a call back buzzed into space. Most likely it had come from Skype or some similar digital provider.

He sat back in his chair, wondering how to progress. Arthur was his best lead; the loose-tongued police chief had more to say and the knowhow to provide Slim with inside details.

But where was this heading? Hired to investigate the possible infidelity of a rich investment banker, he found himself unearthing details of a long-ago cold case, and a number of others around it.

He wasn't getting paid for this. It was best to let it go and forget it. He had rent to pay. He couldn't afford such an expensive tangent.

Yet the same compulsion was drawing him as that which had made him enlist so many years ago now. The need for adventure, for exoticism; it was undeniable.

12

Friday morning, he woke with a hangover worse than any he remembered in the last few weeks, glared at the pair of empty wine bottles in the rubbish bin and then tried to coax himself back to coherency with a large fry-up at the greasy spoon café on the corner of his street.

Ted would be at the beach again this afternoon, but would there be any point going to watch him? It was the same ritual over and over. In any case, Emma had told him to get lost. He was on a hiding to nothing.

He was walking back to his house when his mobile buzzed. It was Kay Skelton, his translator friend.

'Slim? I tried to call you last night. Can we meet?'

'Now?'

'If possible.'

The urgency in Kay's voice swayed Slim. He gave Kay the name of a bar a couple of streets from the café. It would be open by the time he walked there.

Twenty minutes later, he found a barman just opening the doors and switching on the lights. He fought the urge

The Man by the Sea

to get started early, opting for a coffee, which he took to a dim corner and sat down in a booth to wait for Kay.

The translator showed up half an hour later. Slim was on his third coffee, and the line of whiskies behind the bar was threatening to break through his defences.

Slim hadn't seen Kay face-to-face since their army days. The linguistics expert, who now worked an easy desk job translating foreign documents for a law firm, had softened and gained weight. He looked like he ate too well and didn't drink well enough.

Slim was still the only customer, so Kay spotted him straight away. He called to the bartender for a double brandy then climbed into the seat opposite.

They shook hands. Both lied about how well the other looked. Kay offered Slim a drink which Slim declined. Then, with a sigh, as though it were the last thing he wanted to do, Kay pulled a file out of the bag he had brought with him and laid it down on the table.

'I made a mistake,' he said.

'What?'

'This is the transcript. I double-checked the translation, and while I had the meaning right, I screwed up with one small section.'

Kay pulled a sheet of paper out of the file. A red circle highlighted a section of scruffy, handwritten text Slim assumed was Latin.

'This section. Your man is telling something to come back, that it needs to return home. Only he's not.' Kay pointed at a word that was so illegible Slim didn't even try to read it. 'Here. Not 'come', 'go'.'

'Go back?'

Kay nodded. 'Whatever it is that your mark is afraid of, it's already here.'

13

Slim felt numb as he sat in the car across the street from Ted's office near Carnwell town centre. The bulky radio equipment was set up on the passenger seat, but the microphone chip hidden in Ted's jacket was giving off no signal. It had been a long shot, after all, unless Ted was wearing the jacket, but if Ted had left it slung over a backseat there was still a chance it would pick up voices.

The trump card, Slim knew, was to confront Ted himself, but that would set off a storm Slim wanted to avoid for now. If he could just catch a few of Ted's self-absorbed mumblings, it might give him a few clues, and he kicked himself for forgetting the microphone chip Emma had planted in her husband's jacket.

A door opened in the front of the office building, and Ted, briefcase in hand, strode down the steps and made his way around to the car park at the rear. Slim pulled a sunshade across his window and pulled headphones over his ears. He heard only a muffled crackling, followed by the thump of a door closing, which told him at least that the battery in the microphone was still live.

The Man by the Sea

Then the start of a car engine. A moment later, Ted's green sedan appeared on the slip road that led around the office to the car park.

Slim turned around in his seat, adjusting the wire from the headphones so that he could drive properly. As he went to put the car into reverse, an innocuous white Metro pulled out of a space a few cars down from his.

He saw the driver's face in his wing mirror and let out a groan.

Emma.

Ted had turned onto the main road. Emma was waiting for a couple of cars to pass so that she could trail her husband with more discretion. Slim noted it wasn't the car he had seen in their drive; likely a hire car, or, if Emma was really stupid, borrowed from a friend.

Slim slammed his car into gear and pulled out. He couldn't let her follow Ted. Not only would she certainly bungle it, but she risked destroying any chance Slim had of finding out the truth.

The traffic was mercifully heavy for this time in the afternoon. Slim kept Ted's car in sight as it led a line of others up toward a branch onto the coast road, taking his time as ever. With one ear in the microphone, Slim mapped out in his head all the possible routes Ted might take and where he could cut Emma off. It all depended on whether Ted made the first turn, or whether he continued further to another narrower road that intersected with the coast road halfway along to Cramer Cove.

He turned. Two other cars followed, then Emma. Slim gunned the engine, hacking past a van on a blind corner, his heart thumping. A horn blared in his ears as he punched his old car up a rise then accelerated hard down an inclining straight.

The turning which led out to the coast road came up on his left. Slim braked hard, emitting a squeal of resistance from his car, then jerked it across the opposite lane and into a tight opening, barely avoiding an oncoming car, the driver of which looked too shocked even to use his horn.

Slim's attempt to get ahead of Ted immediately seemed folly, as the road wound down through thick forest, flattening out briefly to cross a ford, then rising sharply up through more trees and shadowy, sloping fields. Slim gritted his teeth; it would only take one tractor or a car coming the other way to foil him. With each turn he expected an obstruction, but he made his way without alarm up to the last short straight before the road joined back onto the coast road. He was a couple of hundred metres back when Ted's car drove past.

He stamped the accelerator. His car bumped through a pothole deep enough to crack the chassis on the ground. Slim winced, but he'd worry about repairs on another day.

A second car passed the junction. It was red, the second of the two that had followed after Ted, meaning the first had turned somewhere else.

Through a gateway Slim spotted the roof of Emma's white Metro behind the hedgerow. It was going to be close.

The junction came up ahead. Slim shut his eyes, pulling out blindly, coming to a stop where he completely blocked the road. He didn't dare open his eyes. If he judged it wrong, Emma would slam right into the drivers' side of his car.

He sat there for endless seconds. Then a horn blared.

He opened his eyes. Emma had stopped about ten feet from his car, and was climbing out, face thunderous.

The Man by the Sea

He got out to meet her, closing the door just as she lifted her hands and cracked him across the chest.

'What are you doing, you stupid bastard? I fired you. I fired you!'

Slim tried vainly to grab her hands. 'I can't let you follow Ted, Emma. I'm sorry. Something dangerous is going on. You have to stay away.'

She cuffed him across the face, but he managed to get hold of one of her arms. He hadn't forgotten everything the army had taught him, and in moments he was holding her tight, arms pressed against her sides.

'You worthless piece of—'

Slim did the only thing he could think of that might not start another fight. He pulled her forward and kissed her in a rough approximation of where her lips ought to be.

She moved at the last moment so his face collided with the edge of her jaw. Despite the failure, the sentiment was taken, and when he tried again, this time Emma responded, opening her mouth enough to extend the kiss beyond something casual between friends.

When Emma pulled away again—reluctantly it seemed, this time, Slim said, 'I need time to deal with this. Please. It's important.'

Emma stared. As a peace offering, he pulled from a pocket the hip flask he always carried and held it out. A little something sloshed at the bottom.

'Brandy?'

Slim shook his head. 'Whisky. Supermarket own brand.' He shrugged. 'I'm poor. It does its job. I'm no connoisseur.'

Emma stared at the flask then nodded. She took it,

unscrewed the lid, and took a long swig before handing it back to Slim, who did likewise.

'Can we go somewhere?' Slim asked. 'I need to talk.'

Emma held his eyes. He saw she had put on makeup before coming out, and he already felt part of some big betrayal, as the effort was surely for Ted.

'I know a place,' she said.

14

The fishing shed in the woods not far from the lake was little more than a shack with a padlock on the door. Inside, it was surprisingly tidy, furnished with a bed, a table and chairs, and a few cupboards. Outside, a path wound down through trees to a little lakeside jetty.

'It was in Ted's family,' Emma said by way of explanation. 'His father used it for a retreat. Now I do. I keep it nice. I don't fish, though. Just read books, take walks, and think.'

Slim had followed her car while wrestling with an awkwardness of expectation over what might happen when they reached their destination. Would their feelings have defused or strengthened? As he stood before her, he found himself not caring about Ted or the case. She was a woman, he was a man. Both, in their way, were lonely.

When he finally plucked up the courage to reach for her hand, he found hers already reaching for his.

Later, when they lay side by side, looking up at the wooden rafters where cobwebs drifted on an invisible breeze, following sex that improved, for Slim at least, only a little on the intervening years of barrenness, Slim said, 'I knew you'd cheated on Ted. You recognised the signs to look for.'

'Are you going to judge me?'

'I'm not in a position to.'

'Good. I don't care what you think of me. He knows I'm bored stuck at home, but I gave up a career to keep house for him. He wanted children, I know, but it never happened, and it's too late for me now. He works all hours; what does he expect?'

She was rambling. Slim let her, watching the ceiling while she tried to find excuses for whoever else might have lain with her on this old bed in the cabin by the lake. Slim didn't care; he was trying to figure out what happened from now, and how he lived with the irony of sleeping with a woman who had charged him to expose her husband's infidelity.

'There are no more barriers between us,' Slim said, during a brief pause. 'Can you tell me about your husband when you first met? I want to know if he ever mentioned a former lover. Maybe not even a lover, maybe just a friend.'

'I'll tell you what I can if you tell me why you stopped me from following Ted today.'

'Because I don't want you to disturb what he's doing. If you disturb him, I fear he might stop.'

'And why would that matter? Whatever he's doing, I want him to stop.'

'He's not having an affair.'

'Then what's he doing? Tell me!'

Emma slapped Slim across the face. The suddenness of the action and the unflinching look on her face told him that Emma was a woman who expected to get what she wanted. No matter what it might be.

'I think it's safer if you don't know just yet. I think Ted could be involved in something dangerous, and the less you know, the safer you'll be.'

How could he tell her Ted was trying to exorcise an evil spirit? It sounded ridiculous even to him.

Before she could respond, he added, 'Has your husband at any point mentioned a woman called Joanna Bramwell?'

Emma stared at him a moment. Then, as though forgetting they'd spent the last half an hour having sex, snapped, 'Is that the slut's name, is it?'

Slim shook his head. 'I told you, Ted isn't having an affair. Not with Joanna Bramwell at any rate. She died several years before you and Ted met. In 1984.'

Emma frowned. 'How?'

'She drowned at Cramer Cove. The night before her wedding.'

'What's that got to do with my husband? Unless you think Ted killed her?'

Slim felt the urge to nod, even though he hadn't really entertained the possibility before. After all, as Arthur had told him, there was no evidence to suggest it was anything other than a tragic accident.

'I think it's unlikely,' Slim said truthfully.

'Because he's not a murderer,' Emma said before he could finish. 'I mean, he just isn't. It's not in his blood. He's always been such a gentle soul.'

'You don't have to convince me,' Slim said. 'But I do think they knew each other. I'd like to find out how well.'

'I can ask him.'

Slim shook his head. 'I'd rather he had no idea he was being followed. At least not for now.'

Emma propped herself up on her elbows. 'So, can you tell me why you know all this? How could you make a connection between Ted and this dead woman?'

Slim took a deep breath. 'Because every Friday Ted drives out to Cramer Cove to tell her to leave him alone.'

15

Slim mulled everything over with a bottle of Co-op wine. He had lost Emma at the first mention of hauntings, as expected. She had made an excuse to go home. He wasn't sure if he were sad about that or not. His body still tingled from the sex, but his mind felt a mixture of guilt and resentment.

Just before lunchtime, he got a call from Arthur Davis. They met downtown, in the empty family room of a dirty pub. Arthur was eating chicken out of a basket when Slim arrived. The police chief had already ordered Slim a beer, and it sat getting warm across from him. Slim wondered how long it would be before the chief pulled him for drink driving on principle.

'What did you find out?'

Slim shrugged. 'Not much. People aren't talking.'

Arthur pushed a file across the table. 'Andrea Clark. First victim. October 9th, 1987.'

'Popular time of the year for death, isn't it?' Slim muttered. He sat down but didn't touch the file. 'Drowning?'

Arthur shook his head. 'Fell from the cliffs. Hit her head on the way down.'

'Unfortunate. Accidental death?'

Arthur nodded. 'Andrea was a strong swimmer, swam for her school in regional competitions. She was also part of a crew known for cliff jumping around local beaches. She was seventeen. Anyone who thought they were it in those days got up to such things.

'Cliff jumping?'

'Not off the top. These cliffs are covered with level areas that overhang. Kids love it. Twenty, thirty feet up if you're brave.'

'So what made this a suspicious death?'

Arthur sighed. 'Cliff jumping is one of those things you do for cred. To impress the boy or the girl. No one does it alone.'

'What else? That's purely circumstantial.'

'Her boyfriend at the time gave an interview. He was a suspect early on but had an airtight alibi. He said she'd lost her purse, that she might have gone to look for it.'

'Any truth in that?'

'It checked out. Her purse was found in the seaweed at high tide a few days later.'

Slim watched Arthur's eyes, waiting for the big reveal.

'And there was also this.' Arthur pulled a photograph out of the file and passed it to Slim.

Slim studied it. The picture hadn't aged well, and showed little that was easy to discern at any rate.

'A girl's hands, bloated by too long in the water…?'

Look at those lacerations. I was still a junior officer in those days, but I did see the body. Her hands were cut up really bad.'

'From the fall?'

The Man by the Sea

'From the climb.'

'That makes no sense.'

I had no power in those days,' Arthur said. 'I listened, I learned. But what I saw … it didn't make sense. Years later I came across a similar case in the Cairngorms in Scotland. Man fell into a gorge, had to climb out, but he fell. His hands were ripped up by the rock, though.'

'You don't think she was cliff jumping?'

Arthur shook his head. I think she was trying to climb to the top of the cliff, and she fell.'

'Why?'

'The inquest decided she had got cut off from the beach by the tide. She was trying to climb to safety, but she slipped.'

Slim nodded. 'The evidence suggests that,' he said. 'I can understand how they came to that conclusion.'

'There's more. Let me give you some background to the victim. Andrea Clark was one of the cool kids. She was outgoing, she was strong. Not a shit-taker, if you know what I mean. She played sports, representing the county at tennis as well as swimming. As a junior officer, my role was to investigate her background, and what I found was not a girl who would have panicked at getting cut off by the tide.'

'Fear can do funny things to people.'

Arthur finished his drink and shook his head. 'She was the kind of girl who would have chanced the swim despite knowing the rips. If the water was a bit rough, she might have climbed up to a dry ledge to wait for the tide to turn. She would know it was about six hours. It was October. It was cold, but it wouldn't have killed anyone.'

'Yet she chose to attempt the climb?'

'Have you been out to the cliffs at Cramer Cove at low tide?'

Slim nodded.

'Then you'll have seen how it gets steeper further up. It would take serious balls to take that climb on.'

'I couldn't do it,' Slim said. 'And I was in the military.'

'But if it was your only choice, you would damn well have taken care, wouldn't you?'

'For sure,' Slim agreed.

'So tell me why a girl like that climbed with such desperation that she cut the shit out her hands before falling to her death?'

Slim nodded. Only one answer made any sense. 'Something was after her,' he said.

Arthur said nothing. He just stared at the tabletop, his fingers slowly drumming on the wood.

16

Emma needed him, she said. And Slim needed information, so he did what he had to do.

And it wasn't that bad, not when the gloom inside the cabin hid some of the lines on her face, and he could imagine how she had been, back before time took her best days from her. When they were among the sheets, he talked to her as he had once hoped he might talk to his wife before she ran off with the butcher, touched her where she liked to be touched, caressed her, told her words he hoped were true more than they were, and for a while, he was about to shut out the bad thoughts that seemed constantly craving for his attention.

Emma had brought a flask of tea, although it didn't taste like tea, and Slim considered again that he ought to start cutting back. Perhaps if it were just tea he could focus and think, but Emma seemed less concerned with her original intention for hiring him and more about what he could do for her in bed. To his relief, though, she had brought a large cardboard box along with her, and suggested there might be answers somewhere inside.

It was filled to the brim with paperwork of all kinds: correspondence, piles of old letters, forms, documents, and other odds and ends that Slim paled at the thought of sorting through.

'He brought this when we married, and it has followed us around everywhere,' she said dismissively, as though her interest in the case was waning in place of her interest in him. 'Ted won't notice it's gone, but I'll be picking spider webs from the loft out of my hair for weeks.'

Later, with the box open on his dining table, together with a bottle of red wine he was trying not to drink, Slim balked at what looked like an impossible task. Ted had seemingly kept everything, and a couple of neat stacks of unimportant bank statements and notices still in ripped envelopes, wrapped with elastic bands, showed how far Emma had got with the sorting before giving up.

Thinking about how the second half of the afternoon had gone with barely a mention of Ted, Slim knew the focus had shifted. He was Emma's case now, and the story of Ted and Joanna was his to pursue alone. He sensed this was how life worked for Emma: she cared little for what Ted did while her own idle attention was captured, and assisting Slim now kept him in her life a little longer.

As he glanced up at one of his own bills protruding—half-opened—from his kitchen's rubbish bin, he wondered if it was inappropriate to ask for payment.

He had forgotten to return the borrowed Shakespeare DVDs, and since the fees were already mounting up, he put one on to pass the time while he sorted through Ted's belongings, looking for clues.

MacBeth. He could see the appeal, and felt if it was written in slightly more layman's language he might enjoy the book. It was also clear how someone interested in both poetry and Shakespeare, and who grew up in the free-rolling 1970s, might have an interest in the occult. That the ghost of Joanna Bramwell haunted Cramer Cove seemed without doubt, but where Ted fitted in remained the issue.

Was it really possible Ted could have murdered her?

That a man spouting Latin by the seashore could have killed someone seemed preposterous, but Slim had seen shy-faced bookworms turn into machine-gun-wielding psychos in the heat of war.

Anything was possible when the situation was right.

The bottle of red was done before blood appeared on Lady Macbeth's hands, and Birnam Wood was on the move by the time Slim had figured on a system for sorting Ted's papers. Anything with handwriting on it went in one pile, anything without in another.

As the movie came to an end, Slim wondered whether the shop at the end of his street was still open, and whether his need for both more booze and food was worth the excursion.

In the end, he hauled himself up out of the chair, avoided his reflection in the hall mirror, and headed out. It was just before nine. Sunset was already several hours past, and the wind had got up. Slim, wearing just a light sweater, scowled as he reached the corner and found the shop's lights off and a shutter drawn down.

8.30p.m. He would try to remember next time.

As he turned to start the windy journey back to his flat, a car pulled out of a parking space further up the street and accelerated past him. Slim frowned, and turned to look. On a tight residential street with two lines of parked cars leaving only a single-lane channel, it was lucky the street was one-way. Had the car not accelerated so sharply, he would have paid it no attention, but as it stopped at the junction farther up the street, its brake lights flashing briefly before it pulled out, Slim recognised Ted's green sedan.

17

The radio equipment was still in Slim's car, but he pulled it out and hauled it up to the flat, checking his watch repeatedly, wishing he had drunk less. By the time he'd dumped the equipment on his bed, got it plugged in and switched on, he estimated he had a couple of minutes at best. Carnwell was a twenty-minute drive from Yatton, fifteen on clear roads if you really floored it.

The radio was giving off only a fuzzing, which could have been engine sound, or just dust in the receiver. He needed more to know for certain.

He pulled off the headphones, turned the volume to max, and sat down on the edge of the bed to listen.

He was starting to doze off when he heard the thump. He sat up, jubilant.

A closing car door. It proved beyond doubt that he had seen Ted's car, for here was Ted, arriving home.

Or was it Emma? After all, she, not Ted, had a reason to stalk him.

No other sound came from the microphone, so Slim went into the other room and checked his phone. No calls or messages from Emma, but there was one from Arthur Davis, checking in about their scheduled meeting tomorrow.

The police chief's keenness to hand over details and information regarding the case of Joanna Bramwell and the other dead girls was beginning to unsettle him. Slim, a financially destitute private detective being shoehorned cold cases by the one man with the power to revive them hinted at a greater depth of unwelcome feeling than Slim had encountered so far. What if the residents of Carnwell wanted Joanna Bramwell left alone? What can of worms was he dragging up out of the sand of Cramer Cove?

He was just thinking to retire to bed when his phone went again.

An unrecognised number. Slim picked it up but said nothing, waiting for the other person to speak.

After a few seconds he heard a grunt, then a voice. 'Mr Hardy? You there? Name's Nathan. Nathan Walter. Is this a recorded message? Where to start … Christ.'

'I'm here.'

'Ah, Mr Hardy. You're quiet.'

'It's late.'

'So it is. I apologise for that. Listen, I needed to talk to you. I seen something out on the road—'

'Where did you get my number?'

'I just got picked up, see. Taken in? Chief Davis let me off with a caution, told me if I wanted to run my mouth I should give you a call.'

Nathan belched. Slim suppressed a groan, wondering if it was time to delist his number.

'Why did Chief Davis give you my number?'

'He said Greater Manchester Police had a department that deals with stuff like this.'

The Man by the Sea

Greater Manchester Police? Slim lifted an eyebrow.

'Uh, yeah, that depends. Why don't you just tell me what, uh, happened, the same way you told Chief Davis?'

'He cut me off before I got to say much—'

'Well, I'm not cutting you off. Lay it out. All of it.'

'I was walking my dog along the cliff this evening. Bull Mastiff, takes a lot of walking. You a dog owner, Mr. Hardy?'

'I'm not. Had a cat once. My wife's lover stole it when he stole my wife.'

'Oh, well, anyway, me and George—that's me dog's name—we're up on the cliff and the fog's rolled in. Not unusual that, but we—I mean George and me—we see someone throwing bags over the edge of the cliff. I mean, they could have been disposing of a body, couldn't they?'

'More likely dumping rubbish,' Slim said, wishing he could just end the call. 'Did you see who it was?'

'Nah, looked like he was wearing a big coat. Might have been a homeless guy.'

Slim forced a smile the man couldn't see and resisted the urge to hang up.

'What happened then?'

'See that's just it. I don't know. Fog closed in for a sec and when it cleared he was gone. Like, just vanished. Thought he'd gone over the edge like, but it's sheer right there. Me and George went and had a look but couldn't see nothing down there in the water, not plastic bags, nothing. Like he disappeared into thin air. Think that's what I saw, you know, that ghost?'

'What ghost?'

'They say there's that girl, don't they?'

'What girl?'

'The beach-walker, cliff-walker, whatever they call it.

That one people reckon they see at night, down on that beach. Cramer Cove?'

'Yeah?'

'That's right. Well, I think I saw her. Chief Davis said you were making a documentary. I mean, I'm happy to do an interview. How much will I get paid?'

Slim suppressed a groan. 'That depends. Tell me the exact spot you say you saw this ghost and I'll get back to you.'

'Well, I'm not a hundred percent sure…'

Slim made a mental note of everything Nathan said except his phone number. Whatever he had seen—if anything—it was unlikely to help, but Slim logged it as something to check out anyway.

The phone call over, he retired to the couch with a beer to mull over the latest developments. His head was spinning with a dozen different threads, none of which led anywhere. He was no longer sure why he was involved in the case, now that he had established Ted Douglas was not having an affair—with a living person at least—and Slim himself had graduated to sleeping with Ted's wife. It was an unholy mess which he had somehow become entangled in, but there were people desperate for him to solve it. Whatever else, he was certain that there was murder at its heart.

He was getting up for another beer when a loud thump came from the other room. Ted froze, straining his ears, at the same time glancing around for something to use as a weapon should the intruder attack him.

His eyes had settled on a glass vase on his dining table when he realised he was being stupid. The bedroom window didn't open, and no one could have got to the bedroom without walking right past him.

The Man by the Sea

He had left the microphone on, that was all.

Someone must have got into Ted's car and slammed the door. He went into the bedroom and lay down on the bed, listening. Nothing. He waited, considering plugging in the headphones, when a rustling came from the speaker.

Slim sat up. Someone was in Ted's car. He heard a crackling sound like crumpling paper. It continued for a few seconds before Slim realised it was rasping laughter. A scrapping noise, like nails down a blackboard followed, then the laughter again. The person shuffled around, then came another thump.

The door closing. Slim shivered. He looked up at the window and really needed the curtains closed. He got up and drew them across, and as he went back to the bed, a pop came from the microphone.

He tried the volume dial, but nothing happened. As he checked over the machine, an LED began to flash, indicating a signal failure.

Either the bug had been destroyed, or it had been discovered.

Slim's first instinct was to drive over to the Douglas's house and see for himself what had happened, but he was far too drunk even to trust himself getting down the stairs. His second was to call Emma, but it was nearly eleven o'clock and it might arouse suspicion. In the end he went with the third option, which was to down a large whisky, throw his equipment off the bed and go to sleep.

First, though, he went around the flat, locking all the doors and windows. Something about that laugh … wasn't quite right.

18

He woke after a fitful slumber filled with nightmares. Stumbling into the kitchen, he brewed coffee while he checked his appointments for the day. His answering machine flashed to indicate received voicemails, and he found the first two were from other clients he had left in the lurch after his interest in the Ted Douglas case took off. He scheduled to return both calls later in the day, after finding a red reminder for his electric bill poking through the letterbox.

A third voicemail was from Emma and a fourth from Arthur Davis. Reluctant to hear either so early in the morning, he chewed down a bowl of cornflakes then checked both, listening with disbelief as they related two versions of the same thing.

Ted Douglas's green sedan had been burnt out last night, shortly before midnight. Started with paraffin taken from a lamp in the family's garden shed, there was no sign of forced entry to the car.

Ted Douglas swore he left it locked. Emma blamed

him. Ted blamed a disgruntled client. And Chief Arthur Davis, who had to sort through all the chatter to find the answers, didn't know what to think.

Ted had spent the morning in the police station, but the police had no evidence to support anyone's claim, so as of yet, no charges had been laid. Ted had been upstairs sleeping, and no trace of paraffin had been found on his clothes. Emma, who had been watching TV in the lounge, admitted Ted would have needed to pass her to get outside. When suspicion had fallen on Emma, she claimed to have been on the phone to a friend at the time she noticed the fire outside, something her friend's call log had confirmed.

Ted continued to blame a client, Emma one of Ted's multiple supposed lovers. Arthur's message said he was sorry to cancel his scheduled meeting with Slim over lunch, but he was stuck at the station until the matter was sorted out.

Left with time to fill but not wanting to stay in his flat, Slim headed to Cramer Cove, the bright October sun chasing away enough of the shadows to set his mind at ease while he stood on the wide foreshore with a view across the beach. The sea was choppy today with a westerly wind off the Irish Sea. Seagulls dived and swooped out over the water. Slim tasted salt spray on his lips.

As soon as he took the path up the cliff out to the headland, his unease began to gather. Dipping down into a carved hollow with a thick hedgerow of gorse on either side to keep out the wind, he found himself hurrying past clefts in the trail where it passed blind gateways or stands of scraggly trees. He remembered his military days, early morning patrols through enemy territory, and the fear that was ever present on his shoulder like an angry parrot, ready to scream at him without warning.

That all but one patrol

(a boot and another boot and a bloody stump and pieces and pieces)

ended without alarm only served to worsen the problem. You were forever waiting, building the enemy up in your mind into some terrible destructive beast, so that when it finally emerged, all you felt was a twisted sense of relief.

From the clifftop, the coastline laid itself out in a tapestry of crags and bays. A few miles to the north, the wide expanse of Carnwell Sands and the town tucked up against its shore was in stark contrast to the narrow, enclosed beach of Cramer Cove, with its impassable cliffs, jagged pincers of rocks, and an invisible undertow that had lured several people to their deaths.

Quite the place for a romantic, pre-wedding walk.

It had to be murder. Joanna Bramwell had met a secret lover here the night before her wedding, and whatever had transpired had left her drowned.

That she was supposedly haunting Cramer Cove made little sense, but the evidence was there: the argument existed that both Becca Lees and Andrea Clark had been murdered, even if the evidence was circumstantial at best. Slim wouldn't like to argue it in court, but over a few beers he was certain he could prevail.

And there was a third death, yet for Arthur to explain.

Slim walked to the top of the path, then along to the headland where he found a single lonely bench looking out to sea.

It would make sense that Ted had been involved in all

The Man by the Sea

three deaths. It seemed absurd that he could be a serial killer, but perhaps he had made one bad mistake and had been trying to cover it up ever since. That he would have moved back to Carnwell to be close to a life he wanted to forget made no sense, particularly when the cases were closed, but perhaps there was something pathological about him, and he couldn't keep away.

Slim made a note to ask Emma to check the dates of Ted's business trips dating back to those days, but it was so long ago now it might be impossible to get accurate information.

Or maybe Ted had an associate, or even someone on the payroll. With his money, nothing was discountable, but none of it explained why Ted spent every Friday afternoon at Cramer Cove reading out an archaic banishment spell.

Slim sighed. What he had was a mess, plain and simple.

A cloud had rolled in to cover the sun, and a few spots of rain had begun to fall. Slim started to get up, but then some old military training kicked in, and he froze, moving only his eyes, trying to gauge the danger some sixth sense was warning had found him.

The headland dropped off dramatically up ahead, a steep slope of jutting ledges and scree that became a sheer drop to the ocean, but back the way he had come, the path rose up a gentle slope to where the path branched in two, one fork heading down the cliff to the beach, the other over a stile into a field, where it continued following the coast northward in the direction of Carnwell Sands.

A figure clad in black, face hidden by a hood, stood by the hedge on the other side of the stile, watching him. It was a blur at the corner of his eye, but he couldn't get a better view without turning his head and alerting the stranger to his knowing. Slowly, he lowered himself back onto the bench, but kept his head angled south, as though he were interested in the coastline heading down toward Liverpool.

He let his military instincts gauge the distance. About sixty metres. Even as out of shape as he was, with no cover in either direction for half a mile or more, he would back himself to run the figure down, unless he or she was some kind of athlete.

It was also a perfectly adequate distance for someone with a little skill to aim and fire a shotgun.

The bench was his only cover unless he went over the cliff edge, and that could only end one way. If someone was going to fire on him, they were more likely to try if panicked. If he just got up good and slow, perhaps they would hold their fire.

It would also give him the best chance at getting a clear look at them.

He put his arms on the back of the bench and lifted himself up with exaggerated movements. When he was fully standing, he paused, nodding as he looked out to sea, as though appreciating the view one last time before leaving. Then, with all the speed his military training had given him, he whipped his head around. At the same time, he dropped into a crouch with the bench for cover, and lifted his little digital camera, firing off a burst of photos.

The figure bolted. Slim got one good look at a black-clad shape with a pale oval face framed by thick cords of hair, then it was gone, vanishing behind the field hedgerow, heading north along the path to Carnwell Sands.

Slim stood frozen for more seconds than he would have liked, then dropped his bag and gave chase. Running up

The Man by the Sea

through spongy couch grass he was out of breath in moments, but when he reached the stile and threw himself over, he should have seen the figure running along the bottom of the field, on a path enclosed by a thick hedgerow of rock, gorse, and brambles.

But ... nothing.

Frowning, Slim started down the path. The grass was too short to hide anyone, and the hedgerow dense and almost impenetrable, its purpose of protecting the field from the elements meaning it was too high to be easily climbed. In any case, the angle of its line, sloping around to Slim's right meant no part of it was hidden from view.

So where had the figure gone?

Slim stopped and stood still, listening. There was only the sound of the sea and the wind. No footsteps, no heavy breathing, no shifting of vegetation as though someone was hiding nearby.

Slim shook his head, wondering if he was losing his mind.

Then he remembered the camera.

He put a hand on his pocket, but it was gone.

He spun, heart racing. A glint in the grass near the bench identified it lying where he had dropped it. He could retrieve it, or hunt for his observer. If he left the camera, the stranger might double back somehow and steal it. Slim recognised the same paranoia that had plagued him during his army days, but could do nothing about it. With a sigh, he headed back to get the camera.

Fortune was not on his side. It had fallen on one of the few rocks protruding through the thick grass, and the screen was a spiderweb, unviewable. The memory card was undamaged, and his computer could read it, but that was at home.

A fog bank had appeared out to sea. Within a few minutes it would engulf the clifftop, and while Slim felt comfortable enough out in the open during daylight, reduced visibility was another matter.

With a last resigned scowl aimed both at the vanished watcher and his own ineptitude, he headed for his car.

19

With a lingering unease making him reluctant to go straight home, he stopped in at a local pub where he could leave his car within walking distance of his flat, then used his mobile to dial up his voicemail provider.

Emma had left three messages on his landline voicemail. Arthur had left one, and there was another from Kay.

He called the translator.

'I couldn't stop thinking about that recording,' the translator told him. 'I knew I wasn't quite right with it and I wanted to track down a copy of that book.'

Slim sat up. 'And did you?'

'Out of print, out of stock. Copy on eBay at six hundred quid, but, you know, I'm not that keen. So I did some ringing around the second-hand shops. Most of them had no idea of what book I meant, but one did.'

'You got a copy?'

'No, but the owner sold a copy a couple of months back. Said he remembered the customer well.'

Slim gave a slow nod. The customer could only be Ted

Douglas. If he were ever to get to the bottom of this, he needed to speak to Ted. Until he could find a reason to accuse a complete stranger of a thirty-year-old murder, it would help to know as much about him as possible.

He thanked Kay and took down the number.

20

Slim stayed a while longer in the pub and drank more than he felt was necessary, making banal conversation with a couple of early drinkers, but failing to banish the growing sense of unease that was creeping up behind him. Unable to put off the rest of his life any longer, he walked back to his flat, leaving the car in the pub car park to be collected later. He thought about calling Emma back, calling Arthur, going down to see the bookshop owner, or about thirty other things, but during the walk back he finally made peace with himself.

He was avoiding looking at the photos. It was that same primal fear he remembered from the military: you heard the crunch of a footstep behind you and you wanted to do anything but turn and confront the horror, yet you knew you had no choice, that whatever nightmare lay in wait for you, your life could not continue on its path until it had been faced, and should you be lucky enough to find only a deer or a rabbit or a frightened boy running an errand, part of you would be disappointed that it was not your Room 101, that it was not the worst thing in the world, because you didn't trust yourself to find that same level of courage again.

An off-license lay between his flat and the pub. Slim drank half a quart of good old, liver-shredding navy rum before making the reluctant climb up the stairs to his flat.

His laptop sat on the kitchen table where he had left it. He switched it on, drinking the rest of the rum while waiting for the old machine to load. By the time he plugged in the memory card and sat down, he was so drunk that he had to squint to clearly see the pictures.

He had taken nine shots in his digital camera's burst. Of those, four had missed the subject completely, while another three were so blurred to be of no use. One of the final two was of a black shape turned away from him, but the last shot had caught the figure in profile.

A pale face beneath a hood, looking away from him as the figure started to turn. The picture wasn't clear, and the distance was too great for the computer's digital zoom to improve it, but if he could find a professional to enhance it, he might have an answer.

One thing was certain, though, from the delicate jawline and the angle of the forehead.

The face belonged to a woman.

21

'I've been trying to reach you all day. I need you, Slim.'

From another voice, the same words might have warmed his heart. From Emma they just filled him with dread.

'The fire. I heard about it from someone,' he said, hoping she wouldn't ask who before he'd had time to come up with a believable but uncheckable source. 'What happened? Do the police know anything?'

'There was a local football derby last night. They said it was probably due to a few drunks on their way back from the game.'

'Is Carnwell big enough to have hooligans? I didn't even know there was a team.'

'Exactly. It's a cover up.'

'For who?'

'For whoever is trying to kill me. This dead girl, most likely.'

'Isn't that something of a contradiction? And why burn Ted's car? Why not your house?'

Emma began a rambling monologue about the depraved minds of criminals, none of which made any sense. Slim agreed and disagreed in all the required places, eventually getting her to hang up with the promise of a liaison in a couple of days, once police interest had died down.

The next person he called was Chief Arthur Davis.

'Football hooligans,' Slim said, before Arthur had even spoken. 'You get a lot of trouble after Carnwell Athletic's home games?'

'It was the Cup,' Arthur said, then laughed to confirm it was a quip. 'What time are you free, Slim?'

Slim dropped a cup into the sink. 'I'm sitting in the car with the engine running, waiting to know our point of rendezvous,' he said.

'Tesco's car park,' Arthur said. 'Half an hour. We'll take it from there.'

'I'll be waiting,' Slim said. As he hung up, he remembered his car was still in the pub's car park, a good twenty-minute walk.

~

'Traffic,' Slim said, climbing into Arthur's passenger seat. 'Can't you have a word with the town planning department about building a few more roundabouts?'

Arthur didn't smile. 'We have no leads,' he said. 'She blames him, and he blames someone with no fixed name or address. Hooliganism was an easy explanation for the press.'

'Those hounds at The Carnwell Daily?'

'That's them. But seriously, is there no light you can offer?'

The Man by the Sea

'I heard the arsonist,' Slim said.

Arthur turned to face him. 'You what?'

'I had a bug in Ted's car. Cheap one, non-recordable. I thought I saw Ted's car trailing me, so I loaded up, hoping to catch a door slam, which would have given me all the proof I needed. What I got was that and more. I got laughter.'

Arthur said nothing for a few seconds. 'I'm guessing it wasn't a hooligan.'

'It belonged to a woman. More, I don't know.'

'Emma? We have nothing on her.'

Slim frowned. It would explain the stalking, but it was best if Arthur didn't know they were sleeping together. The laughter, though, it hadn't sounded like Emma. It had been too … wild.

'I can't explain it,' Slim said. 'There's something else, though.'

He pulled out prints of the two best photographs taken the previous day. 'I went for a walk on the cliffs yesterday. Caught someone spying on me.'

Arthur turned them around and peered at them. 'They're pretty grainy.'

'My printer makes them look worse,' Slim said. 'Ink's a bit old, don't use the thing much. It's a woman, that's about all I can tell. I got off these shots before she bolted. Didn't catch her, though. She just ... vanished.'

Arthur squinted. 'I can pull a favour from a friend in the forensics department, see if I can get these enhanced. That face might be identifiable.'

'It looks similar to what I thought I saw by the shoreline a couple of weeks ago. I thought I was drunk or going mad. That's no ghost. That's a woman in an old, water-damaged jacket. I can't explain where she went, but cameras don't lie.'

Arthur smirked. 'Tell that to conspiracy theorists.'

'Those guys are assholes.' He wanted to add that when you'd seen a friend reduced to a pair of stumps in an old pair of boots, no camera double-exposure shared across the internet would ever haunt you again.

'I have a theory,' Slim said. 'But I'm getting ahead of myself. Tell me about the third victim you mentioned before. The old woman. I need all the pieces before I can make the puzzle fit.'

Arthur nodded. 'I can do better than that,' he said. 'I can show you.'

22

Lucy Tanton was an attractive, respectable woman in her forties, the kind Slim would turn down if she prepositioned him on the account that she could surely do better. She smiled at Arthur Davis as though they were old friends, then tilted her head at Slim before giving Arthur a puzzled look, as though the police chief had mistakenly brought an accused to her place instead of the jail.

'I know this might seem a little out of the blue, but I wondered if we could talk to you about your aunt,' Arthur said.

Lucy narrowed her eyes. 'Is there new information? After all this time?'

'A little early to say, but it's possible.'

Lucy let them in. A husband at work and kids at school, she explained, a day off from her own part-time job at a food packaging factory. Just the regular life of a regular suburban family.

'My aunt collected shells,' she explained over tea served

in a cluttered living room where kids' toys had been hastily stuffed into boxes. 'She was something of an amateur artist. She created murals made from sea shells, some of which she sold in local cafes. Despite the warnings and all its history, she liked Cramer Cove because of its shingle foreshore and the fact that it was so quiet. No kids meant rich pickings.'

Slim, whom Arthur had introduced as a friend from Greater Manchester Police, nodded. 'So would I be right in assuming that your aunt, Elizabeth Tanton, was very familiar with Cramer Cove?'

'Oh yes, very. I'd guess she was down there three or four days a week, for hours at a time.'

'And you consider the verdict of accidental death to be incorrect?'

'Of course.' Lucy shook her head. 'It's ridiculous.'

'Her body was found lying just below the high tide line,' Arthur said. 'No marks or anything else inconsistent with drowning, or anything to suggest foul play. The judge claimed that during her search for shells, she had misjudged the speed of the oncoming tide and been caught by it.'

'Ridiculous,' Lucy snapped. 'It makes me so mad just to think of it. Someone murdered my aunt. There's no doubt about it in my mind.'

'There's no way the drowning verdict could be possible?' Slim asked.

'None. My aunt knew Cramer Cove backward. She collected shells. She went down there in a jacket with a bag to collect them in. She wore light trainers that weren't even waterproof. She never went anywhere near the water, and she had no reason to leave the high-tide line. She died in

April, when the water is at its coldest. It's absolutely impossible that she got caught by the tide because she had no reason whatsoever to be anywhere near the water.'

'So what do you think happened?'

'I know what happened,' Lucy said. 'Someone frightened her into the sea.'

Slim was staring at his cup when he heard Lucy addressing him directly. 'You don't seem surprised by that, Detective Hardy. But it's a preposterous claim, is it not? I mean, how could my aunt think she could escape anyone by going in to the sea? Surely she would have tried to climb the cliff or get up onto the lower southern headland? It makes no sense, does it? She was surely murdered.'

Arthur shrugged. 'I oversaw the full police report. There was no evidence to suggest foul play. None. She made a bad decision. That was all that could be given in response to the coroner's report.'

Lucy rolled her eyes. 'And Max.'

'As I told you at the time, a dog isn't evidence of anything.'

Lucy shook her head. 'Perhaps Mr Hardy would disagree.'

Slim steepled his fingers and leaned forward, doing his best to assume the role of consulting detective that had been assigned to him.

'Whether the evidence can be used in a court of law is something I can't assess unless I see it. Then I will pass judgement.'

Lucy went out and came back with a laptop which she set up on a coffee table. She pulled the screen around so all of them could see.

'I compiled this video in preparation for a court

appearance. In the end, my evidence was dismissed, but I always kept it.' She gave Arthur a stern look. 'Just in case.'

The video showed a woman in her sixties playing in a neat suburban garden with a dog, a little spaniel mix. It yapped at her and jumped up when she held out a ball, then rushed off to retrieve her gentle throw. The video cut to a scene in a field where a similar routine played out, then one in a living room with the dog lying on its back while someone tickled it. Delight was obvious from the way it whined and yelped, its tongue lolling.

Just when Slim was beginning to make YouTube comparisons, the video cut again. He sat up, feeling an immediate sense of unease. The same dog, barely recognisable, quivered as it crouched in the corner of a bedroom. Someone was trying to coax it away from the wall, where it was sitting in a puddle of its own piss. The video cut again, this time to a shot of the same dog lying in a basket, eyes wide, whining as someone laid a blanket over it.

'All right, shut it off,' Arthur said, and Slim let out a sigh of relief as Lucy closed the video.

'There's more,' she said. 'But not much. Max died three days later. He squeezed himself into a space between the washer and a kitchen unit and asphyxiated.'

'Jesus Christ.' Slim drained the last of his tea, wishing it contained something stronger. 'What happened to him?'

'Dogs are known to pine for a lost owner,' Arthur said. 'There are a few famous cases. Hachiko in Japan, Bobby in Scotland. But Max, that's not pining.'

'Whatever scared my aunt into the sea also scared her dog to death,' Lucy said. 'I had an animal psychologist examine these videos, and he had no doubt that Max died of fright. Now, what could have done that?'

Slim leaned back in his chair and drummed his fingers the side of his cup.

'Joanna Bramwell,' he said.

23

'We have to begin to consider it,' Slim said. 'There's no such thing as ghosts. That's utter horse-shit. But what if she survived?'

Arthur shrugged. 'If Mick were alive, he would be the man to ask. He never let go of what he claimed, and it killed him.'

'So let's get this straight. We have a drowned girl, dead and buried, who might have been responsible for three subsequent deaths. A man who might have known her thinks he is being haunted and is performing a weekly exorcism ritual. His wife thinks he's having an affair. Someone burned out their car, and while the official line is that it had nothing to do with anything, we both know that it probably did. What the hell is this?'

'It's a mess for sure.'

Slim rubbed his eyes, squeezed them tightly shut, then looked up at Arthur. 'Tell me something. What do you get out of this? For me, it was supposed to be about money. Whether I'll ever see any now is debatable. But you,

The Man by the Sea

Carnwell's chief of police, you could reopen the investigation at any time. You don't need to rely on an internet hack like me.'

Arthur smiled. 'To understand, you need to understand the people round here. The original local people, they're hard northern types who lived off the land and the sea. They say what they mean. They live frugal but honest lives, and their way of life gives pride. To have what is essentially a serial killer in their midst would bring shame to the town. They don't want to know. The sea, it's a wild, untamed thing, and for it to claim a few lives, that's justifiable, but if one among them is committing atrocities, they want to wash their hands of it. I'm not from Carnwell, but too many on my team are.'

'So why help me? I'm already in deeper than I want to be. I was hired to find out if a man was having an affair. This investigation was not what I signed up for.'

'Then why not walk away?'

Slim sighed. 'Curiosity.'

'You have your answer.'

'So what do we do? You know that we need to speak to Ted. If there are answers to be found, he has them.'

'When interviewed about the car fire, he was aggressive with his denial. I fear that he could clam up, and if he does, that's your best lead gone.'

'But what if Joanna Bramwell really is out there, and she's planning far worse for next time than torching someone's car? This woman could be responsible for three deaths already.'

'There is a way we might be able to find out,' Arthur said. 'But it involves a bit of digging.'

'You don't mean what I think you do?'

Arthur nodded. 'The case file has the location of her grave. I can drive us up there.'

Slim gave Arthur a slow nod. 'I need a drink,' he said.

24

A TRAFFIC ACCIDENT REQUIRED ARTHUR'S ATTENTION for the rest of the day. Slim didn't want to stay at home with the pictures in their manila envelope on the table so he took a drive into Carnwell to visit the second-hand bookseller.

Michael Smeeth was an overweight, retired fisherman with a Captain Birdseye beard. His wife's father had died unexpectedly, leaving him the second-hand bookshop on the corner just two doors down from Carnwell's best sandwich shop, which not only provided him with a decent overflow clientele but a hearty lunch each day. Not originally a reader himself, when an accident with the winding mechanism of his main trawl net had forced an early retirement, he had found that limping among the stuffed shelves was quite to his liking, and a sofa in a back room a perfectly pleasant place to slump with a carefully chosen book on a quiet afternoon.

Michael told all this to Slim while waiting for a pot of coffee to brew, coffee he claimed only half-jokingly was 'the best stuff, contraband from an old trawler mate, over on the boat from France, no excise on this beauty.'

Slim smiled and agreed, even though it tasted like any other high street brand.

'I know it must be strange my coming here,' Slim said, trying and failing to fake a London accent. 'You see, I'm a collector of particular types of books. I had my assistant call around to ask about a certain copy, and you were kind enough to say that you had recently sold one.'

'Yes, well, it was an unusual sale, that's why I remembered it.'

'In what way?'

'Well, if you say you're a collector, then the gentleman was surely an enthusiast. The delight he took from finding that book was a little surprising. But then, what do I know? Five years ago I was knee-deep in fish guts for a living.'

'I don't suppose you caught his name?'

'I believe it was Eddie, Eddie Douglas. He said he was from Carnwell, but I have no other details. I'm sure you can find him in the phone book.'

'I'm sure,' Slim said, struggling to keep the excitement out of his voice. 'Out of interest, did he tell you why he wanted the book so badly?'

Michael nodded. 'Oh, yeah. He said he had some trouble in his life, some ghost from his past, and the book was what he needed to get rid of it. To be honest, he came across as a bit of a nutter. I mean, it's just a book, right?'

'Just a book,' Slim agreed. 'But the human mind is a powerful thing, wouldn't you say? Perhaps the book was a crutch he needed to overcome some hurdle.'

Michael nodded. 'Oh, for sure, for sure.'

'Did he say anything else?'

Michael shook his head. 'Not that I recall. He just

seemed so relieved to have found the book he wanted that we exchanged pleasantries for a while and then he left.'

Slim was still mulling this over when Michael asked, 'If you don't mind me asking, what's so interesting about this particular book?'

Slim smiled, preparing his best lie. 'I'm an occult investigator,' he said. 'You might say a ghost hunter. That book is known for its incantations supposed to contact the dead.'

Michael nodded. 'Oh, aye, sounds fascinating. I guess there are plenty of those around here. All the old buildings and everything.'

'Actually, I'm researching a documentary about a particular haunting and several related deaths.'

Michael nodded. 'Ah, you mean Cramer Cove.'

Slim tried to control his surprise. 'You know of it?'

'Of course. Ask any old seaman, and he'll tell you about that place. Haunted, so they say. We used to hate going past there at night. Used to swing back out to deep water if it was a bit choppy, just to avoid it. I mean, no one ever got wrecked, but you didn't want to be the first. Not with her about.'

'Her?'

'Joanna Bramwell. If you're looking for ghosts around Cramer Cove, you must have heard of her. I mean, there's a whole bunch, but if they have a ringleader, it's her.'

'What do you know about her?'

'She died down at Cramer Cove but didn't want to stay dead. Bit of a bee in her bonnet about anyone on her beach. We used to see her all the time.'

'See her?'

'Out on the rocks. You see, in Autumn, the basking sharks come past, and even though they're not predators, their presence in the water drives the cod shoals into shallow water, close to the bays. Rich pickings south of here, so we'd pass Cramer on our way back to the port at Carnwell. She'd be out there watching us.'

Slim felt a familiar shiver down his neck. 'You saw a woman? You saw Joanna Bramwell?'

Michael smiled, as though recalling a fond memory. 'We saw a figure. We were never close enough to see her clearly, but there she was, out on the rocks far beyond where you could get safely from the beach, and far later at night than even a good swimmer would have attempted.'

'At night? Then how did you know what you saw?'

'Trawlers work through the day and night, returning at daybreak with the catch. We'd see her, three, four, five in the morning.'

'But at that time, how could you be sure what you saw?'

'Because of her light. She always carried a lantern. We liked to think she was warning us off the reef out there, but after that first girl turned up dead, we wondered if perhaps she wasn't trying to draw us in. Cramer Cove's very own siren, like.'

Slim could barely contain his excitement enough to line the questions up straight.

'So you knew there was a connection between the dead girl and Joanna Bramwell?'

Michael shrugged. 'Joanna didn't want nobody on her beach, is my guess.'

'Did you go to the police?'

'And tell them what? No one thought of it at the time, not after it was ruled an accidental death. And anyway, the tired dawn eyes of a trawler man aren't much to be trusted. Tired eyes are liar's eyes, isn't that what they say?'

The Man by the Sea

'But Joanna Bramwell might have been a suspect.'

'Joanna Bramwell is dead and buried,' Michael said, with a sudden note of authority that made Slim start. 'What we used to see out on those rocks deep into the night could have been anything.'

'But you said—'

'I told you an old trawlerman's tale. All I know is what I saw, but that light could have been anything, couldn't it? Because what I saw didn't make much sense at the time, I have little hope of it making sense now. If you're done with your browsing, Mr Hardy, I'll bid you good day. I have some boxes to unpack out in the back room.'

Michael's tone had changed. Slim was reminded of new recruits clamming up when asked to report on patrols through enemy territory. The well of initial enthusiasm had run dry, polluted by a creeping fear, and before Michael turned away, Slim caught a glimpse of it in his eyes.

'Thanks for the chat,' Slim said, and headed out, feeling only that he'd added more questions to his growing list.

25

When Slim got home, there were messages on his answer phone from Arthur requesting a call, but when Slim dialled the number, it went straight to Arthur's voicemail.

Emma had gone quiet, so Slim hauled the box of Ted's papers onto his table and got back to sorting through them, vainly hoping he could maintain his concentration long enough to avoid missing something important.

There was no chance of hitting a jackpot, like finding a love letter from Ted to Joanna, and apart from Ted's weekly visits to the beach, there was no other evidence they were even acquainted. Slim's mind wandered as he stacked old phone bills and receipts into one pile, and anything with handwritten text into another. There was little of interest: a few shopping lists, a couple of poor poems lamenting the beauty of the moors and the hills, a few faded flyers for shows and events—one or two of which had dates and times written over schedules—but trying to find out whether these were long-forgotten dates between Ted and Joanna was a headache Slim didn't want.

The Man by the Sea

The Shakespeare company, that was worth a try. If Ted had been a member, perhaps Joanna had, too.

There was something else of interest that it took Slim a moment to notice. Many of the casual notes—shopping lists, telephone call memos, doctors' appointment reminders—were written on headed paper that related to a place called Windwood Animal Surgery.

A search online brought up nothing, but Arthur would probably know about an old veterinarian's that might have closed down. It could have been a part-time job Ted had. Maybe Joanna had worked there, too.

His head aching with possibilities, Slim decided to relocate to the pub up the street for a late lunch. By the time he arrived, he'd already drunk a couple of cans of beer from a local mini mart, and his tongue was soft and loose. He sat at the bar instead of a table and found himself chatting to the barman.

Steven Bennett was greying, overweight, and pale from too long in the pub's gloomy confines. He had grown up in London, buying the pub at the age of fifty, and relocating to Carnwell just a few years before. He knew nothing of Joanna Bramwell, Ted Douglas, or the Windwood Animal Surgery, but he had been an acquaintance of Elizabeth Tanton, who had sold framed murals hung on display in the family room.

'Nice lady,' he said, pouring himself a drink. 'Was shocked when she died. Not the kind of thing you expect to happen.'

'What was she like?'

'In a word? Straightforward. Marches in off the street, tells me where to hang these shell pictures. Tells me she'll be back in a month to collect profits from any sales, and to provide more if I need them. Writes down on a sheet of paper the name of each picture and how much it'll cost me, then tells me to add my profit over the top.' He chuckled. 'I couldn't say no. I had no interest in the stupid things, and I probably sold no more than five or six in the couple of years she was showing up, but she was such a caricature I looked forward to the day she visited each month.'

'She kept regular habits?'

'Oh, yeah. Showed up on the first Monday of every month, always at the same time. Parked in the same spot. Always ordered a cup of black coffee with one brown sugar cube.' Steven chuckled again. 'Always dropped it in the cup with her left hand, gave it three quick stirs with her right. I remember once I decided to play with her, and said we'd run out of brown and only had sachets of white. You know what she did? Laughed my ass off later. She held up a hand and said, 'Hold the coffee this month,' in this posh voice like she was Audrey Hepburn or someone.'

'And what did you think when she drowned?'

Steven tutted. 'Load of rubbish. She 'just decided' to take a swim?' He gave a vehement shake of the head. 'Elizabeth Tanton didn't 'just decide' to do anything. She wasn't an impulse person at all.'

'So you think she was murdered?'

'Oh, I wouldn't say that. I mean it's possible she slipped and knocked herself out, and the tide washed over her and caused her to drown. It's just not likely. Not for a woman like her. I reckon she was pushed.'

'Murdered then?'

Steven shrugged. 'I guess if you want to put it like that. Seems more likely, but what do I know?'

'And her dog?'

'The dog, what about it?'

'I heard it went a little wild after she died.'

'Understandable,' Steven said. 'They'll do that, dogs will. Nice thing, it was. Little spaniel thing, Cocker, maybe, not sure. Used to sit under the bar and drink some water while we talked. Couldn't believe it bit through its leash.'

'It did what?'

'Overheard a conversation, going back a few years now. Lad off the forensics team on the local force was having a going away do. Running his mouth a bit, strangest thing he'd ever seen as a copper and all that. Said they found Elizabeth Tanton's dog running loose up the top of the beach, head lolling, eyes wild. They actually thought it was rabid, until they found its leash near the water's edge. Leather. Chewed right through.'

26

Slim parked his car beside the tree that had just dented the front bumper and stumbled up the path into the woods to the cabin, where he found Emma waiting.

She would say nothing at all until they had finished sex, attacking his body with a relish that made Slim a little uncomfortable. He was already starting to tire of her, but she was the best chance he had of getting close to Ted.

'I want to know as much as I can about your husband,' he said, lying with one arm around her shoulders, his head still spinning. 'You said he was a poet. I mean, no one earns money from that. How did he get by?'

Emma shrugged and rolled away from him, appearing disinterested. 'He did what everyone else did, I suppose. He worked part-time jobs. Shops, that kind of thing.'

'Did he ever work at a veterinary clinic?'

'A vet?'

'I found some notepaper with an emblem on it.'

'Oh, that. His mother's practice.'

'Really? Ted's mother was a vet?'

'Yeah, Windwood Animal Surgery. It was in the high

street. She sold it when she retired, but the new owners screwed up the accounts, went bust, and closed it. Ted's mother always out-earned his father. The old man resented it until he died.'

Slim nodded. So that explained the blotting paper. 'Another thing. Was there a Shakespeare company around here? I found some flyers.'

Emma was quiet for a few seconds. 'Not that I recall,' she said, frowning. 'I mean, there might have been, but if there was, I don't know of it. Mind you, a lot of Ted's life before we met is a mystery. His involvement with this slut, Joanna Bramwell, for example.'

'I'm trying to find out how they might have known each other,' he said.

'Why not ask him? I think the time for secrecy is about done.'

'I'm worried that he won't want to talk to me.'

Emma rolled her eyes. 'Well, of course he won't. You're going to figure him out, and he'll know that.'

'Figure him out?'

'Yes. That he's planning to kill me and set it up like it was done by some ghost, like he didn't know anything. And then, I'll be mown down like an unwanted dog and no one will suspect a thing.'

Emma was rambling, looking for sympathy. Slim wondered if she had been drinking too. 'Why would he want to kill you?'

'Because he wants me out of the way. He hasn't loved me for years.'

'Why not just divorce?' Slim patted her stomach. 'It's clear you don't love him too much either.'

Emma rolled away. 'You don't understand.'

Slim didn't, but he tried to act like he did. 'It's an honour thing for you, isn't it?'

Emma sighed. 'My parents divorced. I promised myself I would never fail like they did. Sometimes, what you see on the surface is different to what lies beneath.'

'That's true.'

'So, is there anything else?'

Slim considered what he ought to tell Emma. She had begun to intrigue him, not least because she held various levels of anger and resentment toward her husband, but because he sensed she was hiding something, something that perhaps she wanted to reveal. The few drinks he'd had on the way over made it easier to loosen his tongue.

'I did find something,' he said. 'An insurance letter.'

It wasn't a lie. He had found a shopping list scribbled on the back of a reminder for a home contents insurance bill.

He waited. Emma had tensed, and he heard a long expulsion of breath.

'I know what it might look like, but it was just my way of bringing a debate to an end.'

'Go on,' Slim said, having no idea what Emma was talking about, and praying she didn't call his bluff. 'I might need to know.'

'Ted has a habit of investing in some of the firms he deals with. He makes money because he sometimes knows in advance where the market is going. This time he got it wrong, and we almost lost the house. He wanted to gamble, thinking he could cover it. I didn't trust him. We had a joint insurance policy due to pay out when Ted turns sixty-seven, but he has a heart condition and might not last that long. I forged his signature to cash it in early.'

'I see,' Slim said.

The Man by the Sea

'When he found out, he hit the roof. He's never forgiven me. He doesn't care that we needed the money to cover the debt he made. He just goes on about me wanting him dead.'

'I think that's a little over the top.'

'Is it? He's angry because he knows I have a separate policy of my own. It matures in five years, but if I die, it pays out big.'

'I see,' Slim said again.

'Do you? Do you really? Because you know what it means, don't you?'

'What?'

'He talks up my dislike for him, but it's rubbish. This, though, is something. It means Ted has a genuine reason to want me dead.'

27

Slim left Emma with her paranoia under the pretence that he had errands to run, but really he needed somewhere to get drunk, and in his own way try to make sense of everything. He felt up to his neck in a barrel of confusion, and no matter how strong the urge to walk away, he knew there was no escape.

Allocating the day as a day off, he got roaring drunk, ignored all calls, and stumbled homeward sometime after dark, waking up in a park in the grey light of pre-dawn, his keys caught in the frayed fabric of his pocket's inner lining, and a vague memory of being unable to get into his flat.

He went up, cleaned and showered, changed his clothes, then swallowed enough ibuprofen to take the edge off his thumping headache.

For the first few hours of the day, he went through the box of Ted's old papers, looking for something that might back up the information Emma had freely given him, but found nothing useful at all. Suspicious, he checked the dates on as many items as were dated and found nothing later than 1992.

The Man by the Sea

Had Emma responded to his lie with one of hers? If they were playing a game, he wondered who was playing the cat and who the mouse.

Just before lunch, he headed up to Cramer Cove to wait for Ted. He parked up the road out of sight where he usually parked, afraid of spooking Ted. Then he went to wait for Ted in the trees just inside the broken gate leading onto the beach.

It was approaching three when he decided Ted wasn't coming. Emma had mentioned a hire car Ted was using for work, but for whatever reason, Ted had decided that this Friday would be the first he missed since Slim had begun his weekly vigil.

Slim called Arthur and asked if there were any updates on the photographs, but Arthur hadn't heard back from his contact. Instead, Slim got to thinking about how he had seen the figure up on the cliff, and it had just vanished into the air.

Ghosts vanished, it was true, but ghosts didn't get caught on camera, and people didn't just disappear. They went somewhere.

Always.

He headed up the cliff path, keeping an eye out for anyone following him, but he felt alone on the windswept headland, with the sun beaming overhead chasing away any shadows. He reached the stile into the field where he had seen the figure, then climbed over and followed the footpath, sticking close to the line of the hedge.

It appeared an impenetrable tangle, at its heart an old stone wall that had partially collapsed over the years beneath an accumulation of soil and plant matter. At times, farmers had added sections of fence or barbed wire to keep animals in, the rusting remnants of which were now buried beneath a thicket of gorse, brambles, and couch grass.

Somewhere in the distance, a siren was wailing as Slim knelt down by a section of hedgerow, looking for the signs of animal trails: fox burrows, badger sets, anything that provided a way through the thicket. Beyond was a section of cliff not accessible by any way other than getting over the hedge, a section also impossible to reach from the beach, even by clambering out over the rocks at low tide. Slim had seen it on maps, but perhaps this section of rugged coastline could offer him answers.

Working from the stile down, Slim got on his hands and knees and peered under the hedge, trusting his military instincts to know what he was searching for. He remembered lying in the dusty, scorched dirt of Iraq's eastern provinces, fingers searching for hidden entrances and trapdoors, feeling for strange edges where they should be curved, the give of wood where there should only be rock. There was always that feeling of reluctance, of hoping you found nothing, that you returned from the mission with nothing of interest to report, because, when you found something, the problems really began.

A thin trail led into a patch of dead brambles. Maybe the roots had been eaten through. Slim lay on his front and reached in, feeling around for how far the trail went inside. His fingers had just closed over something cold and hard when his mobile rang.

He sat up, pulled it from his pocket, and answered.

'Where are you?' Arthur Davis said.

'On the cliffs.'

'Get here, now. Ted Douglas has had a serious car accident. He's on his way to hospital as we speak.'

28

Ted had crashed on his way to Cramer Cove, failing to make a sharp turn at the bottom of a hill and slamming straight into a tree that had both crushed the front of his car and trapped him inside. A police cutting crew had removed him, and an ambulance taken him away.

Three police cars, a tow-truck and a handful of gapers remained on the scene when Slim arrived. He saw Arthur taking measurements around the back of Ted's crumpled car, but ticker tape kept everyone unofficial a few metres back from the crash scene. Slim waited with other onlookers while the police carried out their investigation.

The road descended a steep hill with a tight, near-ninety-degree turn at the bottom. Tire tread marks on the road showed where Ted had started to make the turn, then tried to correct himself, and hammered into the trunk of the gnarled old tree, around which the hedge had grown like a protective barrier.

The police had drawn chalk lines around everything, marking a couple of spots with reflective triangles as though they could make sense of Ted's decision with mathematics.

With little to see, the crowd slowly dispersed. Slim, feeling a little conspicuous as the last remaining onlooker, retreated down the road a little way, in the direction Ted would have gone had he made the turn. The horizon between Cramer Cove's cliffs was a blue V rising above a green and brown line of trees, hedgerows, and fields, with the road winding down the centre of the valley on one side, then snaking up the side of the valley on the other, disappearing over the top of the rise.

Something crunched underfoot.

A handful of bits of shell lay in a neat pile beneath his shoe. Had it been cockleshells like the poem he might have smiled, but it was simply a few limpets and periwinkles, with a tiny, shining conch in the middle.

He looked back up the road. Ted's car could have started around the bend, viewed this very spot, then swerved back away, hitting the tree.

Arthur was standing beside a police car, shaking his phone, then angrily waving it in the air to look for a signal. Slim waved him over. Arthur said something to a colleague, then wandered across to where Slim waited.

'What happened?' Slim asked.

Arthur shrugged, shaking his head. 'We won't know until Ted wakes up. If he wakes up.'

'That bad?'

'I was in the first car on the scene. He was in a bad way. Unconscious. A lot of blood. I'd guess he lost control as he made the turn. Perhaps he was going too fast.'

'Looks like he tried to turn out of it.'

'I guess we'll have to wait for the full report.'

A couple of other officers were throwing looks in their direction.

'A problem talking to me? I can make myself scarce.'

'I said you lived nearby. Might have seen or heard something. I can't stay long. We'll talk later.'

'Can you go back into the files for the three dead girls?'

Arthur frowned. 'I think so. Why?'

'I'd like to read the complete description of each body.'

'I told you the cause of death.'

'Not that. The circumstances in which they were found, position of the body, objects found nearby. You have photographs?'

'Some, yes.'

'If you can get copies, I'd appreciate it.'

'It sounds important.'

Slim shrugged. 'It could be. I don't know yet. In your opinion as Police Chief, what do you think happened?'

Arthur sighed. 'With a road like this you're always playing the averages, especially if you're used to big, looping A-roads or all the lights in the city. Ted got a bit cocky, took the downhill straight a bit fast, botched his brake and turn. Not the first I've seen.'

'And you really think that?'

'I told you, as Police Chief. I'll wait for the report.'

29

Emma was heartbroken, but not heartbroken enough to show up at Slim's flat with a bottle of wine. She cried before and after sex, while during, her face held a look of concentration that suggested she was going through the motions but little else.

'Someone tampered with his hire car,' she said. 'Maybe they cut the brake wires, I don't know, but they made him crash.'

Slim didn't point out that car brakes weren't like bicycle brakes, but the assurance in Emma's expression meant he could rule her out.

'It's quite hard to tamper with a car to that degree,' Slim said. 'It takes a lot of expertise.'

'Do you think there was someone else in the car?'

'Not unless they escaped unscathed,' Slim said. 'The police report will be able to tell us.'

'What about Ted? Will he be okay? I mean, we had our differences, but I don't want to see him—' She burst into tears. Slim consoled her for a couple of minutes, then called a taxi to take her to the hospital.

Just before she left, Slim asked her to wait a moment while he went into another room. He returned with a battered teddy bear which he held out with a sheepish grin.

'Can you give him this?' he asked, his cheeks reddening from apparent embarrassment after he had given them a sharp pinch on his way back.

'What is it?'

'It's my lucky charm. I spent a little time in a military hospital after getting hit by shrapnel. A local kid gave it to me.' He smiled and patted it on the head. 'We've been a long way together, haven't we, mate?'

Emma smiled. 'That's sweet. I'll make sure he gets it.'

She slipped the bear into her bag. Slim didn't remember where it had come from--some phone company's free gift or whatever--but it headed off to the hospital with Emma, and the little recording chip he had pushed into the hollow space behind its plastic eye went along with it.

Alone again, but half drunk, Slim called Arthur. 'Make sure Ted's under guard,' he said.

'Why?'

'Let's just say I'm cautious. Also, see if you can keep a record of anyone who comes to see him. His wife, obviously, but also any friends, neighbours, work colleagues.'

'Sure.'

'It would be good to know what kind of affection Ted Douglas commands.'

'Right.'

'And do you remember what you told me the other day? About Joanna Bramwell?'

A pause. 'Yes.'

'I think it's time we found out once and for all if Joanna Bramwell is truly dead.'

30

Arthur picked Slim up at 11 p.m. from outside the closed corner shop at the end of Slim's street. No longer in his police uniform, Arthur was dressed all in brown and driving an old blue Ford Escort. After stopping at a petrol station for takeaway coffee—'To steady the nerves,' Arthur said, his hand trembling as much as Slim's often did as he took the coffee and flashed Slim a smile—Arthur drove them across town and parked down a leafy farm lane just outside the town limits, then they walked the last mile to the graveyard along a public footpath leading through fields. Arthur refused the use of any light during the awkward, stumbling journey, stating that it wouldn't do for the chief of police to be caught opening graves, so they moved much slower than they might have done, tripping on roots and ploughing through thickets of brambles until they were both thoroughly miserable.

When they had reached the graveyard, tucked away behind a church built low into a valley and overrun with grass, Arthur led them to a plot near the back and a granite headstone that had begun to list. In the torchlight

Arthur now allowed, Slim read: *Joanna Bramwell, 1960-1984, taken too soon, forever beloved*.

Then, from a deceptively small pack, Arthur withdrew a set of metal poles, which he began screwing together.

'No shovels?'

Arthur shook his head. 'We can avoid that mess, I think.' He held up the instrument. 'This is what people in these parts used to use to drill for water. A smaller version, obviously.'

The object was a long, thin drill. The hollow shaft was an inch wide, each section two feet long. They could be screwed into each other, while on the top side of each was a fitting for a cross-piece handle three-feet wide. It allowed for both Slim and Arthur to work at once, pulling one side each, then passing the handles over. A specialist screw-drill head fitted onto the end.

Arthur chose a place at one end of the plot, drove the drill's metal tip into the turf, and looked up at Slim.

'Let's see if we can find oil,' he said.

Half an hour in, Slim wondered whether using shovels might not be less strenuous. His shoulders and back felt torn open, and it seemed as though they had only gone down a couple of feet. But as the drill handle got close to the ground, and Arthur removed the handle to add another two-foot length, he realised they were now four lengths in. Six feet. Wasn't that the standard depth for a coffin?

A few minutes later, Arthur paused. 'Did you feel that? That momentary give?'

Slim felt only muscle ache, but Arthur was convinced they had reached the decomposed remains of a coffin.

'Now we come to the tricky part,' he said. 'We have to get the shaft out without collapsing the hole we just made.'

The Man by the Sea

Inch by inch, they wound the drill back out again, removing each section of shaft as it came. When the drill head appeared, Arthur replaced it with a new flat-headed piece. It was hollow-ended, but by the light of their torch, Arthur explained how inverted hooks could be used to spear something and hold it like a fish on a line.

Again, far slower than Slim's shoulders appreciated, they lowered the now-blunt-ended drill back into the hole. A couple of times, they met resistance, and Arthur grimaced, explaining his fear that the shaft had collapsed and they would have to start over, then they pushed through, and the drill continued down. At last they reached the depth they had previously reached.

Arthur called for a halt and looked up at Slim. 'Now we need one solid push,' he said. 'I hope you're feeling okay. If this comes up with nothing, we're starting again.'

Slim forced a smile. 'Let's get this done and get home.'

'Three, two, one—'

They leaned on the shaft handle with all their strength. It plunged another hand span before hitting resistance.

'Right, let's pull her up, Arthur said.

They withdrew the shaft from the ground. Arthur unscrewed the end and laid out a piece of cloth. Then, turning the length of shaft upside-down, he inserted a metal rod into it and pushed out the contents caught inside.

In the torch's light it looked like just a few lumps of soil to Slim, but Arthur laughed.

'Got her,' he said. 'First time. See that?' He poked a lump of material that unfolded into a rough diamond shape. 'That's cloth. Which means this,'—he pointed to another lump beneath—'must be tissue. And this little piece here that looks like gravel, that's a section of bone.

I'll get this sent away, and we'll have an answer in a couple of days.'

Slim nodded, feeling a sense of elation nearly swallowed up by his disgust at what they had done. Together they tidied up, and then ruffled up the grass where their feet had been to make it harder to tell anyone had ever been here.

As they walked back to the car with their treasure wrapped in a plastic bag, Slim should have felt excited. Instead, even though the night wasn't that cold, he found himself shivering.

31

After getting up late the next morning, Slim drove to the hardware store on the outskirts of town and picked up some better recording equipment so he could leave the microphone feed to Ted's hospital room running while he went out. To his surprise, his credit card wasn't yet maxed, but he hurried back to his car anyway, before the store clerks realised their error and called him back.

With Ted still in intensive care, and, according to Arthur, unable to receive any unsupervised visitors, there was no hurry to set it up, so he took the box of Ted's papers down to a local cafe, where he tried to sort through them while resisting the urge to relocate to the pub across the street and get drunk.

As he delved deeper, he kept coming across the same things. Innocuous notes written on veterinary surgery notepaper and receipts for shipments of medicine he guessed were for animals, dull bank statements, and simple, handwritten photocopies for local Shakespeare productions.

But on one, he found a phone number.

The production's date was March 1st, 1982, at a local theatre the internet told him had burned down in late 1985. That a thirty-five-year old phone number would still work was too unlikely to be true, but an online database gave him a historical address.

When he knocked on the door, he didn't expect to find the same occupant who had lent their contact phone number to a local Shakespearean society, but the house's middle-aged owners had kept in occasional contact with a lady called June Taylor, a retired English teacher now living in a care community complex not far outside Carnwell.

When he made the call, Slim decided to be straight up with June, and told the kindly-sounding, well-spoken lady that he was trying to track down an old friend.

June invited him right over for afternoon tea.

Glad he'd managed to stay sober for nearly a full day, Slim drove over, bringing the leaflet with him.

He had to sign in at a central security desk, and was informed by a guard that, for general security purposes, his visit may be interrupted. Then he was led to a third-floor corridor and a door at the end. Through a fire door window he saw a pleasant view of hills and a lake glittering between them.

The door opened. June Taylor peered up at him from a wheelchair, then gave him a welcoming smile more deserving of a long lost son. Her face was lined but kindly, like a familiar towel.

'So nice to meet a fellow thespian,' she said. 'Won't you come in?'

The guard left them alone and returned to the downstairs reception. Slim followed June into a small living room where she had already prepared a tray of tea and biscuits. Warmth emanated from every corner: the photographs of family lining the shelves, the colourful throws over the sofa, the little table in front of the window with its collection of ornamental teddy bears.

'I'm afraid I haven't cleaned,' June said, sounding genuinely apologetic, even though the place was spotless. 'I wasn't expecting company until tomorrow, when my son will visit.'

Slim suddenly felt like a fraud. Sitting in this delightful room with this charming old lady, a hangover still gnawing at the back of his skull and an army of lies on his tongue ready to march out in procession, he fought an urge to confess like a gum ball that needed spitting out.

'Um, Mrs Taylor—'

'I got out some old pamphlets,' she said, picking up a bundle by her feet, and the dice was left uncast. 'You're an old friend of Ted's, aren't you?'

'I knew him from school,' Slim said. 'But I moved away and we lost touch. I had this flyer lying around, but that's my only link to him. I know it's likely to get me nowhere, but it was a place to start.'

'I'm afraid I haven't seen him in years, not since he left the club, not long after this. It was shortly after Joanna died, actually. My, my, Ted was heartbroken.'

And there, just like magic, a link. Slim took a slow breath and concentrated on getting the flurry of words on his tongue out in the correct order.

'Joanna was his girlfriend?'

June gave a fervent shake of the head. 'Oh, no. But any fool could see they were perfect for each other. Any fool except Joanna, who had that other man she planned to marry.'

The way her tone dipped suggested distaste. Perhaps June had a more romantic view of the world than Slim did.

'She was beautiful?'

'Oh, an oil painting. You'll never have seen a more beautiful lady in all your life. She could act, too. She certainly had a career ahead of her. Here, this is her.'

June held out a pamphlet. The front picture showed an ensemble cast at the front of a stage at the end of a performance. Creases obscured some faces, and one third was faded from a folded side left too long in the sun.

In the centre, though, the two leads shone resplendent, their smiles filled with confidence and joy.

'This is her?'

'Joanna? Yes, that's her. The best Juliet I ever produced. And that's your friend, Ted.'

He was barely recognizable from the stooped, morose figure Slim had watched through binoculars for the last two months. His arms were held aloft as though he could carry the weight of the world and laugh off all its problems.

The title read *Romeo and Juliet*.

'Ted was the lead?' Slim asked.

June smiled fondly. 'They had such chemistry. Everyone could see it. We were never a huge company, but our performances always did well. We were selling a thousand tickets a night for our last couple of shows, and I'm sure a lot of that was down to Ted and Joanna. I was thinking we might do a tour. Then Joanna died, and Ted was so broken up by it that he quit and moved away. We carried on for a few years, but it was never the same. I could never find two leads with quite the same magic.'

'And you don't know what happened to Ted?'

June shrugged. 'I believe he moved south. If he came

The Man by the Sea

back, I'd never know. He has certainly never come to visit. I don't think he could. Too many memories and all that.'

'Joanna?'

'He was devastated. He was like a wrecking ball. The night after she died he broke into the club and ran amok, breaking props, destroying costumes, burning scripts. I knew it was him because I caught him at it. I could have pressed charges, but I didn't have the heart.'

'You say Joanna died?'

'She drowned at Cramer Cove, the night before her wedding. Such a tragedy. Shocking.'

'And you don't believe there was any foul play?'

For the first time, June gave Slim a look of exasperation. 'I'm a romantic, but I'm also a realist. The coroner's report was conclusive. I haven't the foggiest idea what she was doing down there. Likely no one does. I know she did like to practice her lines outdoors. Maybe that was it. For some reason she fancied a swim.'

'You don't think Ted—'

'Not for an instant. He was besotted. Absolutely. And afterward, the Ted we had known, the fantasist, the dreamer, was gone. It's not a lie to say that part of him died with Joanna. So, Mr Hardy, when you finally catch up with him, he might not be the man you remember.'

Slim nodded. 'A lot of time has passed. You said they weren't a couple? I did hear a rumour elsewhere that Ted was married. I don't know about children.'

June nodded. 'He was an attractive man. It's likely he settled for someone. Many of us do, even if the love of our life might have eluded us.' She gave a fond smile. 'I was married to my old Jim for forty years, rest his soul. A wonderful, loving man, but steady as an old bus. I rarely felt that ... oomph after the first couple of years.' Her eyes twinkled, and for a moment the years fell away. 'There was someone once ... but that's another story. I won't lie that the reason I cast Ted and Joanna as the leads was as a shameless attempt to match-make. We were all in on it.'

'So what happened?'

Joanna had an old boyfriend from college she had agreed to marry sometime before she joined the company. Turner, he was called. That was his first name. A bland nobody, worked in taxes. But Joanna was stubborn. She had agreed to his proposal, and it would have been too messy to break it off. I know what she felt for Ted. I had her crying on my shoulder one night.'

'About Ted?'

June nodded. 'About everything.'

'So she planned to go through with it.'

'Absolutely. Even though we both knew she was turning away from true happiness.'

'If you don't mind me asking, where was Ted on the night Joanna died?'

'I believe he was at home. He was of course interviewed by police, and he claimed to have been home in his room, practicing his lines for our upcoming production along with a taped version of Joanna's. His mother told police she had heard voices into the early morning.'

'What about the boyfriend? What was his name ...Turner? What happened to him?'

June shrugged and shook her head. 'I didn't know him well so I can't say. His fiancée, I'm sure he was distraught. It was a tough time. I heard he moved away and later married. I saw him around town once with a couple of children. I think Turner got over Joanna and moved on.

Ted, he might have gone through the motions, but I don't think he ever got over Joanna. He can't have.'

'Why do you say that?'

'You can't understand, and I can't explain it in a way that would make you, but Ted and Joanna ... they were like halves of the same soul. And they realised it too late.'

32

Worried he was tiring her, Slim bid June farewell and headed home, his mind swirling with emotions he couldn't have expected.

So, Ted and Joanna had known each other, possibly even been lovers. Joanna's death had devastated Ted, causing him to give up his dream of working in the arts, move south, and end up working a dull office job.

Back at his flat, Slim switched on the radio link to the bug he hoped was now in Ted's room at the hospital, then scrawled his ideas down on a sheet of paper. Another link had formed, but there were so many doors yet to close. The book and the Friday visits to Cramer Cove had taken on a greater significance. Ted, a fantasist and dreamer, in June's words, believed Joanna was haunting him. And the nature of his words—*forgive me*—suggested he harboured a responsibility for her death.

More missed calls had come in while Slim was with June. Arthur, saying he had procured the crime scene photos. A manager from Ted's former company, stating they held no such records for employee business trips, but

The Man by the Sea

that if they did, they would be classified company information anyway. And two from Emma, saying she was afraid and needed to see him.

Slim got back to sorting through the box of Ted's papers, but the deeper he delved, the less he felt he would find anything. It all felt sanitised, as if Ted had removed anything of any use, leaving only junk: shopping lists, bank statements, receipts for local restaurants, notes for reminders of tennis matches, memos of missed phone calls from double-glazing companies.

Slim poured himself a whisky and began writing down all the dates he could find. Something, somewhere had to hold. Ted was the acting, poet son of a respected local vet, and Joanna Bramwell, engaged to be married to Turner, he of the first name, was Ted's unrequited love. She had drowned at Cramer Cove on the night before her wedding while Ted practiced his lines for their upcoming performance of Romeo and Juliet. In the intervening years, Joanna's supposed ghost had been seen on multiple occasions, and three other drownings at Cramer Cove could be linked—circumspectly, at least—to her. There was even a rumour that Joanna had survived her supposed death, and Ted, at least, believed she was haunting him.

Slim skim-read a receipt for horse-tranquilliser, and felt like head-butting the nearest wall.

There was something, just out of reach. Not an answer, maybe, but at least a clue. Perhaps Arthur's pictures would shed some light. Slim stood up to go to bed, almost knocking over his glass on his unsteady feet.

'I miss you...'

Slim coughed, his chest tightening. He spun looking for the source of the voice, saw only the recording device he had left on.

'I miss you, too.'

Slim stumbled as he moved toward it, tripped, and hit his forehead on the edge of a chair.

Pain bloomed. He rolled onto his back, clutching his face, as a gravelly voice repeated over and over:

'Never leave me ... never leave me ... never leave me...'

33

'Visiting hours closed at eight. And the hospital confirmed there was no one in Ted's room after that time other than scheduled doctors and nurses. It's also impossible that he spoke because he's still hooked up to a ventilator that he couldn't have removed by himself.'

'Then I'm going insane.'

Arthur smiled. 'You and me both. There was nothing else?'

Slim shook his head, a gesture which sent judders of pain through him. His own visit to the hospital this morning was still fresh in his mind, even though he had been released with a clean bill of health and the advice to drink less.

'I knocked the machine when I tripped and disconnected the receiver. It's like there's a conspiracy against me.'

'I got you the pictures,' Arthur said. 'I'm still waiting on the DNA guy, but the enhanced photos should come back tomorrow.'

He slid an envelope across the table. Slim sighed as he took it.

'You know, there are times I want out of this mess,' he said. 'This isn't what I was hired for. I'm broke. I'm not getting paid for this. I want to walk away ... but I can't.' He shook his head. 'Not until I know.'

'If this is really Joanna Bramwell, back from the dead?'

Slim gave Arthur a weary smile. 'Something like that. Hopefully before she decides she has a bone to pick with me and lines me up in her crosshairs. Right let's take a look at these.'

'Are you going to tell me what you're looking for?'

'Only if I find it.'

Frowning, Slim shuffled through the photographs of Andrea Clark, Becca Lees, and Elizabeth Tanton. Those of Elizabeth, the most recent of the three, were clearest, but those of Becca, the youngest, were most harrowing. At least she looked peaceful in death, her eyes closed, almost a smile on her lips.

Slim looked over each, moving the close-ups to one side and focusing on those showing the whole scene.

'Goddamn it, it's there,' he said.

'What?'

He pointed at a photo of Andrea, lying face down. A handful of shells lay in a crease of her clothing, scattered like someone leaving the first handful of dirt at a loved one's funeral.

'What did the report find in Elizabeth's pockets?'

Arthur lifted a sheet of paper. 'Just a handful of broken shells she was collecting for her art project.'

'Did the report mention what variety?'

'I'm afraid not.'

'I doubt broken shells would be useful, would they? Not for a serious artist like Elizabeth Tanton?'

'I suppose not.'

'And look here.' Slim pointed at the sand beside Andrea Clark's head. 'That grey area? Anything in the notes say what that is?'

Arthur shook his head. 'Nothing. Just part of the beach.'

'It's not part of the natural beach. Look at its colour. In some parts of the world, spotting an unnatural line in the sand can stop you getting your face blown off.'

'I guess you would know.'

Slim was quiet a moment, remembering the time he had failed to spot one, and its consequences.

'Look.' He retrieved a jar from his bag, then unscrewed the lid and upended the contents onto the tabletop.

'Been beach combing?'

'I picked these up off the road near Ted's car accident.'

'A handful of broken shells?'

Slim nodded. 'A handful of broken shells, similar to those found in the vicinity of the previous three people to die at Cramer Cove. You know what this is, don't you?'

Arthur nodded slowly. 'It proves it, doesn't it? It'll never stand up in court, but still, it's proof they were murdered.'

'And by the same person. What I think is that this is the calling card of a killer.'

Arthur didn't buy it, Slim was sure, but it made perfect sense in his mind. Sure, it was tenuous, and had little value in court, but it was another link. With no evidence in the photographs of Joanna's body that the same calling card had been left, it meant her death could be disassociated from the other three.

And that opened up a terrifying possibility.

There was no change in Ted's condition, according to Arthur, who was in regular contact with the hospital. He remained unconscious, hooked up to a ventilator.

After bidding Arthur farewell, Slim called Emma, and met up with her in Ted's family's fishing cabin. She had wanted to meet at his place again, but with paraphernalia from the case strewn everywhere, she would ask questions for which he had no answers. Meeting her in public, too, was a risk; it was possible, in the light of Ted's accident, that his estranged wife might attract journalistic interest.

Slim didn't waste any time telling her what he wanted to say.

'I think you should leave town for a while,' he said. 'If you have family down south, could you perhaps stay with them?'

'I can't,' she said, as Slim had expected. 'You know I no longer love Ted, but how would it look for me to abandon him?'

'I think you should seek police advice,' he said. 'I don't believe it to be safe in Carnwell for you. Not until everything is cleared up.'

He didn't specify what he meant, but Emma shook her head. 'I'm not running away,' she said. 'And what about us?'

'If someone is after Ted, I'm not sure if I can protect you,' he said, deflecting the main thrust of her question. Their relationship was a situation he needed to address soon, but for now it could wait.

'Do you think his accident was just that, or something else?'

Slim shrugged. 'I was informed by the police that it's not uncommon for accidents to occur on that stretch of road. At the moment they're not treating it as suspicious, but they haven't concluded the investigation yet.'

Emma shrugged. 'It was a new car,' she said. 'He'd had that sedan for years. I don't think he was used to the new one yet. His foot might have hit the wrong pedal, who knows? It happens.'

Slim nodded. 'It looks like an accident,' he said.

Emma nodded. 'I actually feel happier, knowing that.'

They had sex, then parted company, Emma to run some errands, Slim to return to his flat, where he found nothing to do but get drunk and sit in front of the television. There wasn't much on, so he put on a DVD he had forgotten to return to the public library, and sat watching Romeo and Juliet while waiting for a bolt of inspiration to strike.

He was avoiding what he needed to do, but if he were honest with himself, he hadn't been this scared since his days on active duty. His discharge from the military had been an embarrassment, but he didn't miss it. Knowing there were sniper sights and booby traps with his name on them had never made for easy sleeping, and now he was getting too close to a possible serial killer for his liking. If the ghost of Joanna Bramwell was an angel of vengeance swooping down to ruin the lives of Ted Douglas and his family, it might pay to stay out of her way.

On the screen, Romeo was drinking poison. Slim frowned as the music blasted him with an aural assault of melancholy.

He had taken up private investigating because it looked easy. For someone used to hunting booby traps, it was no problem at all to uncover affairs and frauds.

Had he known he would end up investigating a

possible triple-murder, he would never have returned Emma's call.

Juliet was just waking up from her coma to find Romeo dead. Slim watched with idle fascination as she first burst into tears, and then stabbed herself.

'Crying shame,' he muttered, as the two families reconciled, and then the credits rolled.

He was walking toward the bedroom when he noticed a small piece of paper lying on the floor.

A receipt.

Handwritten numbers on one side.

10st1lb. 37g/90ml. 19h.

Slim gave a slow nod. Frowning, he folded the paper over and went to the table. He opened up his laptop and called up the internet.

No connection.

Slim groaned. He picked an unopened letter out of a basket and ripped it open.

A telephone and internet connection final reminder. The cut off date was two days ago, and he hadn't even noticed.

Slim was yet to join the smartphone generation, but there was a hotel at the end of the street he had passed with a couple of computer terminals in the lobby he was sure he could use without suspicion. If not, perhaps the public library was still open.

He headed out. As he had hoped, the hotel had free internet, and the terminals were set up in a corner away from the reception desk.

His searches pulled up a string of PDFs heavy on science terminology, and before long, Slim's head was spinning from new information as well as drink. It was difficult to be sure if there was any weight to his theory, but it was possible that Ted Douglas had known the same doubts. After all, if Slim was correct, Ted's failure had shaped everything.

Lost in a mire of drink, exhaustion, and science, it was only when a police car with its siren wailing raced past outside that Slim realised he was dozing. A moment later, a concierge was tapping him on the shoulder, asking whether, if he had finished, whether another guest could use the computer.

With a mumbled apology, Slim collected his things and shuffled out into the night. He leaned against a lamp post and pulled out his old mobile, but after a moment, realised his idiocy. He had let the battery run dead. He had a dozen calls he needed to make, but there was nothing he could do now. In the morning he would try to find an expert to back up his theory.

Farther up the street, a siren was still wailing, and lights flickered above the rooftops. Slim quickened his pace, and just as he turned the corner into his road, he saw a blurred, running shape coming toward him.

'Slim, thank god,' Emma gasped, throwing herself into his arms.

He pushed her away. 'What?'

He looked past her shoulder at the fire engine crouched in the middle of the street between two lines of parked cars, like a fat, red locust.

'I needed to see you,' Emma said. 'I came round, and saw smoke coming through an open window. I called the fire brigade. Oh god, I thought you were in there.'

Slim pushed past her. 'No…'

Water still cascaded through a broken front window, but the hoses had done their job. No sign remained of the fire besides a triangle of black ash stretching up the wall.

'Hardy, you drunk clown!' came another shout, then two firemen were holding back Slim's downstairs neighbour as he shook clenched fists, his face red with anger. 'Look what you've done!'

A couple of police officers sauntered over, and with a stern word banished the neighbour back behind a ticker line.

'Are you the owner of this flat?' one asked.

Slim shook his head. 'I don't own it. I'm just the tenant.'

'Not particularly clever to go out with your cooker left on,' the second said. 'You'll need to contact your landlord and have them contact us.'

Slim rubbed his eyes. 'What happened?'

'You left a hob on, and those boxes of cereal beside your cooker … looks like they fell over.' He nodded to Emma. 'It's lucky your friend showed up, Mr Hardy. Sorry, madam, I forgot your name?'

Emma flashed a look of alarm at Slim. If there were a police report, she didn't want them associated.

'Ah, Kate,' she said. 'Kate Mellor.'

'Well, Ms. Mellor here likely saved you a criminal damage charge, Mr Hardy. It looks worse than it is, but it's still pretty bad. Your kitchen is gutted, but the rest of your place just has smoke damage and now needs mopping up. Your landlord should have building insurance, but I trust you were insured for your contents?'

'Yeah,' Slim said, having no idea whether or not he was. 'I appreciate what you did here.'

'And your flat will need a new door,' a fireman said, coming over. 'It was locked, so we had to force it.'

Half an hour later, after promising to show up at the local police station in the morning to complete a fire

The Man by the Sea

report, Slim found himself on the pavement outside his building with only Emma for company.

'I don't know what happened there,' Emma said. 'I had a brain freeze. I don't know where that name came from, but if it gets in the papers that I was seen with you while my husband is in hospital—'

She looked on the verge of tears. Slim put an arm around her shoulders and gave her a gentle hug.

'It's okay. I doubt they'll need a statement. I'm the one in trouble, but thanks to you, it wasn't as bad as it might have been.'

Emma shrugged. 'I just needed a shoulder to cry on, that's all. I feel so stupid.'

Slim forced a smile. 'You feel stupid? Look at me. I nearly burned down my whole building.'

'What are you going to do?'

Slim shook. 'See if the hotel at the end of the street will take my credit card, I guess.'

Emma pulled out her purse. 'Listen, I wish I could ask you to stay at mine,' Emma said, pulling out a couple of crisp fifties. 'It just wouldn't look good. Here. I know I still owe you for your work.'

Slim made a half-hearted attempt to refuse the money, then took it and slipped it into his pocket.

'Thanks,' he said. 'I appreciate it.'

Emma had parked her car a little further up the street, so she gave him a lift back to the hotel. She kissed him on the cheek before he got out, whispering, 'Be careful, Slim. Try not to drink so much.'

The hotel staff seemed unconcerned that the man freely using their internet terminals just a couple of hours before was now asking for a room, but five minutes later,

Slim, feeling wearier than weary, was emptying out his pockets and pulling off his jeans.

He slumped back on the bed, hands behind his neck, wondering when his world had begun to unravel, whether it was just this evening when he had left the cooker on and gone out, or whether it had started before that, perhaps when he had taken on the case of Ted Douglas, or perhaps even earlier still, when his wife ran off with a butcher, or even when he took his first drink.

Now, his world was slipping out from beneath his feet, and he had no way to prevent it.

He wanted to forget about Ted Douglas and Joanna Bramwell and walk away, but it was too late. His life was linked to theirs in the same way theirs had once been linked to each other. They were bound by an invisible rope, and if he tried to cut free, everything would fall apart.

The police had told him he could return to his flat in the morning, but it was the last place he wanted to go. Darkness waited for him there. Not for the first time, he looked at the small pile of his belongings he had emptied out of his pockets. And he saw again what he had seen the very first time, and he remembered the fireman's words.

He would need a new door. They had been forced to break it down because he had locked it on the way out. Except that he hadn't locked it, because among the pile of his things, there was no key, and now that he thought about it, he quite clearly remembered leaving it on the table beside his disconnected telephone.

So among the many questions that Slim had, the most important right now was, if he hadn't locked his front door, who had?

34

The firehoses had caused more damage than the fire, and Slim found an angry note nailed to the remains of his front door from his downstairs neighbour, demanding the details of Slim's insurance company.

Most of the damage had been done in the small kitchen, where the box of Ted's papers had managed to move itself from the table to become a heap of ashes at the foot of his burned out cooker.

His recording equipment was untouched, as was his laptop, although it had taken a drenching and didn't respond when he tried to switch it on. The keys he had left beside it were gone, as was his flash drive, which he had left plugged in to a USB port.

Slim was trying to fit a warped phone head back into its cradle when the remains of the front door creaked behind him, and then a voice said, 'Slim, we need to talk.'

Arthur looked grey, ten years older than he had at their last meeting.

'You look like you're having a worse day than me,' Slim said.

Arthur just frowned as though he had eaten something bad. 'It's time to start believing in ghosts,' he said.

'I already do,' Slim answered. 'Yesterday I very nearly became one.'

Arthur didn't smile. He pulled up a chair and sat down grimfaced among the wreckage of Slim's flat, an image that was so absurd it brought a smile to Slim's face.

'What's so funny?'

Slim shrugged. 'Everything.'

'I don't think it's a laughing matter.'

'You think what you like. If I don't laugh, I'll probably commit suicide. My life literally couldn't get worse unless someone shoots me in the balls. What did you find out?'

'The DNA test on the forensic sample we took from Joanna's grave came back. It's not her, Slim.'

'What?'

'The DNA is an almost perfect match to a girl called Nellie Taylor, reported missing in Manchester in May, 1982. She had all the traits of a wasted life: a drug problem, brushes with the law, time spent working as a prostitute. She was officially pronounced dead in September 1990, but that's not our problem.'

'I can't believe it. The body in that grave doesn't belong to Joanna Bramwell.'

'She could be alive and well and walking the streets.'

'With a rising headcount under her belt. And you know what, I think I know why.'

Arthur looked genuinely surprised. 'How?'

'For once I got lucky. But I need to speak to a professional to be sure. In the meantime, if Joanna Bramwell really is out there, we need to find her. You need to organise a manhunt.'

Arthur shook his head. 'On three closed cases and a car accident? No way I'll get authorization.'

'And two counts of arson. Ted's car and my flat.'

Arthur looked down. 'We need to talk about that.'

'Please don't say you believe I started it?'

'You're a bumbling idiot, but I think even that's past you. Take a look at these.' Arthur held out his phone. 'Crime scene photos. See this chair? It's lying on the floor. I talked to the firemen who were first into your flat, and they told me it was propped up against your bedroom door. They couldn't be sure if it was blocking the handle or not. They said it might have fallen that way after the fire started, knocked by the shockwave when your cooker exploded.'

'So what they think is that I blocked my own bedroom door before I went out, leaving the cooker switched on and locking the door behind me?'

'That's about it. Unfortunately, being drunk at the time gives you little leeway for reasoning with them.'

'I wasn't that drunk.'

'Goddamn it, Slim, you stink even now. Can't you sort yourself out?'

'I was getting there when Emma Douglas called.'

'Emma?'

'She needed to know if her husband was cheating. I did what I was asked. No, the bastard wasn't cheating. He was reading exorcism rites to his dead lost love. Only she's not actually dead, but she is extremely upset with what he did, to the tune of three dead women and a few close calls, including mine.' He looked up, tears blurring his vision. 'How can I not drink, Arthur?'

'I found one,' Arthur said.

'One what?'

'One of the porters on duty that night in the morgue when Joanna Bramwell's body was brought in. You fancy some fresh air? I think it's time we got you out of here.'

Slim rested his head in his hands and rubbed his temples with his palms. 'Do I have a choice?'

'You know you don't. My car's outside.'

35

They drove in silence. Slim guessed that Arthur was growing weary of the case, a reflection of his own thoughts. They shared a collective fear of what they were uncovering, and Slim felt certain he could have told Arthur to turn back and the police chief would have done so without a word. Now that it seemed likely Joanna Bramwell was alive, Slim wasn't sure he wanted to find her. What kind of a monster the years had made her become ... he wasn't sure he wanted to know.

'Three men were on duty that night,' Arthur said as they drove. 'The coroner, and two porters. The coroner died of heart failure in 2002. Both porters are still alive, but one was old even then, and is now in a care home in Liverpool, suffering from late stage dementia. The other, Paul Edgar, at that time a trainee, now does factory shift work. I tracked him down through our employee database, and he agreed to speak to us.'

'He just agreed?'

Arthur looked pained. 'I had to apply a little pressure. If what we believe is true, he could be facing prison time. I told him I would guarantee protection from prosecution if he came clean about what happened that night.'

'And he agreed to that?'

Arthur nodded but didn't say anything for a long time. Finally, he said, 'Mick died over this. Mick was a good friend.'

Arthur drove them to Barklees, a small town about an hour from Carnwell. After entering the town limits, he checked his car's navigation system, then took them to a shabby block of flats with a view of the distant Pennines. Everything about the area suggested the poverty line was rarely out of view, and Slim wrinkled his nose with distaste as he got out of the car.

'Nice area,' he said. 'I might come house hunting as soon as I'm served my eviction notice.'

'It's this one,' Arthur said. 'Third floor.'

The concrete steps felt heavy underfoot, and the stairwell stank of vomit and stale cider. Slim felt an overwhelming sense of foreboding even before their knock went unanswered. They looked at each other across a door of scratched and faded paint, a number hanging loose and a letterbox crammed with circulars.

'You sure this is the right place?'

'I did a tap on his phone number. This is his address. I'm certain of it.'

After getting no answer for a couple of minutes, they knocked on the flat next door and were greeted by a sour-faced woman who spoke with a cigarette hanging from her mouth, as though she had forgotten it was there.

'You after Edgar? What are you, debt collectors? You know he ain't got anything in there of value, don't you?'

'We're police,' Arthur said, flashing his badge. The woman noticeably straightened.

The Man by the Sea

'Well, he'll likely been sleeping. He works nights at Farnwich Foods.'

'When did you last see him?'

The woman shrugged. 'Week? We're not friends.' She didn't elaborate.

'Does he usually forget to collect his mail?'

The woman shrugged again. 'He's a cranky old sod. Lets it pile up to keep the cold callers away. But he's in there, all right.'

From somewhere back in the flat, a child's cry of anger was accompanied by a crash as something fell over. The woman gave the two men an apologetic look, then headed inside. Arthur saved her a moment of awkwardness by closing the door for her.

'Let's take a look,' Arthur said, bending down to pull the stuffed flyers out of the letterbox. When it was clear, he lifted the flap and peered inside. 'Paul Edgar? Are you in there? Are you—'

His words cut off abruptly, and he looked up at Slim. His mouth wrinkled as though chewing over ideas that refused to organise themselves into speech. As Arthur held Slim's gaze, he turned the handle and the door swung inward. As the hall was revealed, leading to a little living room with the curtains closed, Slim saw what Arthur had seen.

A pair of legs poked out from behind an upturned table. The stench of drying blood came on pungently, making Slim cover his nose and mouth.

'I smelled it before I saw it,' Arthur explained. 'Don't touch anything, Slim. This is a crime scene now.'

They made their way inside, Arthur going first, Slim standing where Arthur told him to stand, moving forward only when Arthur told him to do so.

The body of a man in his late fifties lay face up, his mouth still open in an expression of horror, dead eyes wide, staring skyward. Drying blood plumed around him, dark and oily, in stark contrast to his pale face, as though all the colour had drained out. Both wrists had been cut, and a thin hacksaw lay near one hand.

'Suicide,' Arthur said. 'Too clean to be a murder.'

'How will you explain our presence here?' Slim asked.

Arthur puffed out his cheeks. 'I'll think of something,' he said. 'I know a few guys in this district. I can pull some strings.'

'What are you doing?' Slim said, as Arthur scooped up a handful of papers from an adjacent desktop.

Arthur grimaced. 'I'm removing evidence. He left us something, Slim. Oh my, holy heaven and God. Look.'

He held out a sepia photograph of the naked upper body of a woman lying on a table looking up at the camera. Slim's first reaction was that she was beautiful. Curls of hair haloed around her, and striking eyebrows framed wide, inquisitive eyes.

'Slim. Oh my, look at this.'

Slim took a second picture from Arthur's hand. It was similar to the first, but the woman's head was slightly tilted, and someone had scrawled in red marker across the bottom: *are you haunted yet?*

'Ah...'

Slim turned at Arthur's cry. The police chief had dropped two similar pictures onto the floor. One landed in the blood, and the woman's face was quickly turning crimson. Arthur's attention, however, was fixed on a fifth photograph, which he held in both hands.

On this one, someone had written: *you are now, aren't you?*

Slim stayed at the woman's face. 'Wow,' he said.

In this picture, her eyes had flared, and her head lifted up off the table. Her lips were curled back in an expression of utter hatred.

'Quite the shock when you think someone's dead, isn't it?' a voice said behind them.

Both men screamed. When Slim turned around, the corpse of Paul Edgar had lifted his head, and dark eyes watched them out of a sickly pale face.

36

'We were taking routine photographs,' Paul Edgar said, his voice echoey and ephemeral. He had shaken off their offers of help, and still lay where Arthur and Slim had found him. 'For the files. We didn't notice she was alive until she came at us.'

'What happened?' Arthur said.

'We were terrified. We genuinely thought she had come back from the dead. She was mumbling, unable to speak except in grunts and growls. We panicked, and we beat the shit out of her, beat her unconscious. Then Mick and Dave took her.' Paul's eyes flicked to the ceiling and back to the wall. 'Lord forgive us, she had come from the sea, so they threw her back. They took her down to the cliffs off Cramer Cove, and they tossed her in the sea.'

Arthur sniffed. 'Mick always said ... he always said she came back.'

'We were still wondering what to do when a stiff came in. Runaway, died of an overdose. No personal effects, no identification. It was easy ... easy to fudge a few forms. I let

The Man by the Sea

Mick and Dave do it. Signed it where they asked me to sign.'

Paul closed his eyes. Slim was thinking he had passed away, when his eyes snapped open again. 'I took those photographs, and I have looked at them every single day since. I always wanted to say sorry to her, to apologise for what I did. She haunts me, Joanna Bramwell, she haunts me to this day.'

With a sigh, Paul lay back and closed his eyes again. Slim and Arthur waited a long time, neither saying anything. Finally, Arthur reached forward and held a palm a couple of inches above Paul's mouth. 'He's gone,' he said, shaking his head. 'We need to go, too.'

They returned to the car in silence. Arthur opened the front door, then leaned over and vomited into the grass verge. When he was done, he waved at Slim to get in, then stood outside, making phone calls for a few minutes. Slim watched him pace up and down, passing the phone back and forth from hand to hand, the other making circuits of his face and hair, unable to stay still.

When Arthur got in, he turned to Slim and said in a cold, hollow voice, 'Now, I want you to tell me your theory about how she ended up like that.'

Slim nodded. 'We need to see a vet,' he said.

'What?'

'I need to know if what I think happened is possible.'

Arthur's face was pale. 'Let me make another call,' he said.

37

'I have to say, this isn't the kind of question I have to answer every day,' Rick Harris said, twirling a pen in his fingers like an amateur acrobat. 'Nendril Hydrate was something of a stain on our proud profession.'

'Tell me about it, please,' Slim asked the retired vet sitting on the sofa across from him. Arthur, having set up the meeting, was waiting outside in the car, making phone calls, no doubt still trying to pull increasingly tangled strings.

'Well, it was marketed as a cheaper anaesthetic to what was being used at the time. You've heard of horse tranquiliser, I expect?'

'A little,' Slim said.

'It's a powerful drug used during operations on animals. Its chemical name is ketamine, and unfortunately, it's used by a lot of young people for recreation. It became something of a fashion back in the Nineties.'

'I've heard of ketamine,' Slim said. 'It's like ecstasy, is that right?'

'It has similar effects,' Rick said. 'Euphoria, an out-of-body sensation. Hallucinations if you take too much. Nendril Hydrate was an early version. For a while it was very popular, then problems began to appear. People—farmers, mostly—started to complain.'

'About what?'

'Animals were showing behavioural problems. It took longer to detect in non-human subjects, but eventually we figured it out.' He lifted his spectacles and squinted at Slim. 'Brain damage.'

'What kind of behavioural problems?'

'They varied. But, among others: aggression, a propensity to solitude, nervousness, erratic activity, loss of appetite.'

Slim leaned forward. 'This might sound like a strange question, but what would be the effect on a human?'

'Similar to those of ketamine, but worse.'

'Would it be possible to render a victim comatose to the point where they appeared dead?'

Rick Harris looked uncomfortable. 'Comatose?' He let out a slow breath. 'It's very possible. Ketamine users have this thing they call the k-spot. If you take too much, you find yourself rendered inert for hours on end, unable to move or respond. Without research, I couldn't tell you exactly, but I believe that, yes, it's very possible. Is this what your research paper is about?'

Slim remembered the lie they had told to get Rick to talk to them. 'Yes,' he said. 'The effect on humans.'

'Well, I guess it's possible. Just to clarify, I wouldn't advise you to try it. Not ever.'

38

'Ted drugged her,' Slim said. 'He bought this Nendril Hydrate, and he got her to drink it. His plan was that Joanna would miss her wedding, and perhaps then reconsider.'

'And how did he get her to drink it?'

'They were rehearsing for their production of Romeo and Juliet. She had to drink poison in the end scene. My guess is he conveniently had a bottle of something to hand to use as a prop. He drugged her, then he took her to Cramer Cove, where he left her on the foreshore.'

'She was wet.'

'It rained that night. Check historical weather records. I'd put money on that it did.'

'The voices his mother heard?'

'It wasn't just Joanna on a tape. It was both of them.'

'Why didn't he go back for her?'

'My guess is that he did. He just didn't figure for how early some people walk their dogs. He was confronted by a police roadblock and forced to go back.'

Arthur shook his head. 'It sounds—'

The Man by the Sea

'Plausible. Admit it. Remember, this is Ted Douglas the wannabe actor. The poet. A hopeless romantic. It might sound ridiculous to you or me, but say Ted overhears his mother talking about Nendril Hydrate, about how it knocks animals out for hours, and gets an idea. He orders some using his mother's veterinary clinic's account—the receipt was with his papers—then intercepts the delivery. He drugs Joanna, then takes her to Cramer Cove, a place wild enough to appeal to the romantic in him yet also practically far away enough that if Joanna awoke earlier than anticipated she would still have no chance of making her wedding on time.'

Arthur nodded. 'Yet he gets it wrong. He gives her too much. She appears dead to dog walkers, her body so cold even the police are fooled. Then she wakes up, struggles to escape, scares the crap out of Mick, the coroner, and his crew. They panic and fight her, then faced with what they think is a dead body all over again, they dump her in the sea.'

'And the sea, it seems, likes her. She wakes up on the beach at Cramer Cove with no recollection of her identity yet a desire for solitude as well as violence.'

'And somewhere over the years, she sees Ted again, has a vague memory of what had happened, and wants her revenge. Ted thinks she's come back from the dead, wants to protect his family from what he thinks is her attempt at revenge, and the romantic Ted resurfaces. He tries to exorcise what he thinks is her haunting spirit from his life.'

Arthur nodded. Slim nodded too.

'So where is she?' Arthur said. 'And how has she avoided discovery all these years?'

'I think I know,' Slim said. 'Come on. It's time we found her.'

39

The light was starting to fade as they climbed the path up to the headland overlooking Cramer Cove. They had brought torches just in case, but as they reached the top, the sun broke through a line of clouds and bathed them in a welcoming orange glow.

'This way,' Slim said. 'It was over here, under the hedge.'

So much had happened in such a short period of time, that Slim had nearly forgotten what he had found under the hedgerow on the clifftop, just before Arthur's call to inform him of Ted's accident.

He followed the path to the place he remembered, marked by a twisted oak sapling bent back into the hedgerow by the wind. While Arthur watched, Slim lay on the ground and pushed his way into the hedge. At full stretch, his fingers closed over the hard edge of a wooden board.

'Got it,' he said.

'Got what?'

'A way through.'

The Man by the Sea

He felt along the edge of the board, which was damp and crumbly through age and exposure. Just as he was about to give up and try to get a better grip, his fingers touched metal.

A clasp, the kind found on climbing ropes. It felt grainy and rusty, but when he maneuvered his fingers around it, he felt something threaded through, a piece of metal coil.

'It's tricky,' he muttered, fingers trying to gain purchase. 'Just a little ... more.'

The clasp opened and the coil slipped free.

The effect was immediate. The board sprung up about fifteen inches, revealing a dirt path underneath the hedgerow, like an animal trail. Slim crawled into it, pulling himself through. When he had scrabbled his way out the other side, he turned and called for Arthur.

'Where'd you go, Slim?'

'The other side. Crouch low. I'll pull you through.'

Two minutes later Arthur was wiping dust off his shirt as he sat beside Slim on the grass. Ahead, the land dipped away sharply, ending in a rocky cliff edge. Beyond it, the sea crashed and churned far below.

'That's quite the secret passage,' Arthur said.

'Someone practiced with those clasps could be through in a matter of seconds,' Slim said. 'It only took me a while to figure out because it was the first time.'

'Where did she go from here?'

The hedgerow sloped around toward an inlet valley, but it made no sense for Joanna to go that way. Slim stood and walked to the cliff edge.

It dropped off almost sheer, jagged and deadly. A hundred metres below, the sea hassled a jutting cluster of rocks.

'No way anyone's getting down there,' Arthur said.

Slim shook his head. 'She did, somehow,' he said. 'Let's take a closer look.'

'There isn't anywhere closer!'

Slim ignored him. He lay down on the ground and shuffled on his belly to the very edge of the cliff. His stomach grumbled as he looked over.

'There.'

'What?'

A couple of feet down, a wire ladder hung fixed to the cliff face. It looked like the kind more commonly found on alpine trekking trails, with steel bolts securing it to the rock. For the last few feet, a climber had to rely on a couple of rocky outcrops for handholds, so it had easily remained hidden.

'She went down that? You've got to be kidding me.'

Slim remembered his military trading. 'A lot of things are possible with practice.'

'But why would she? I mean, why here?'

'I don't think she chose this place,' Slim said. 'I think it chose her. I think that after your friend and his colleagues threw her in the sea, this is how she got out.'

40

'I NEED TO SPEAK TO YOU,' SLIM SAID. 'EMMA, IT'S important.'

'What is it about? I was going to head over to the hospital to check on Ted for an hour or two.'

'Have you given any more thought to going south for a while?'

There was a pause. Then: 'No. I don't care what this thing or person or whatever is, I'm not going to let it scare me away.'

'I've asked Arthur to have someone watch your house.'

'I appreciate it, but the locks are quite secure.'

Slim sighed. Emma, despite being aware of the growing threat, was digging her heels in.

'Well, why don't you come to my hotel?'

He could almost hear her smile. 'I guess I could, if it's not too much trouble .... I know you're busy.'

They made small-talk for a couple more minutes, then Slim hung off. He didn't really want to see her, but he could at least make sure she was safe.

He went back to his flat before meeting her, to collect

his recording equipment. In the dark space that stank of smoke, he felt like a thief in his own flat as he collected his things by the light of a torch.

The hotel room was cramped, so he set the equipment up inside the only closet, unplugging an adjacent fridge and using the plug for his power cord. He switched it on, but heard nothing except a low hiss of emptiness with the occasional clump or bang, probably a doctor or nurse moving equipment around. Emma had told him there was no change in Ted's condition. Her husband remained unconscious but stable.

Slim set up a mic and left it running, but there was nothing further to hear. He thought he heard the sound of a car starting up, but he was already a couple of beers deep, so it could have as easily have come from the street outside. About twenty minutes later, Emma knocked on his hotel door. Slim shut the cupboard to make a little extra space, then let her in.

'I'm not supposed to be in your room,' she said, giving him a mischievous smile. I sneaked past the reception while the server was busy with another guest.'

Slim tried to find the enthusiasm to be happy to see her, but all he could see was a ladder leading down a cliff face and a line of dead women lying on a beach.

'I think your life is in danger,' he said.

Emma rolled her eyes. 'Joanna Bramwell? You really think—'

'I have proof she's alive. And while I don't yet have hard evidence, I think she was involved in the deaths of at least three women and responsible for Ted's accident.'

Emma lifted an eyebrow. 'Vengeful spirit, indeed.'

'I'm worried she'll come after you. I also think she could be behind the fire in my flat. Did you see anyone?'

The Man by the Sea

Emma shook her head. 'No, no one who stood out. To be honest, I wasn't concentrating that hard. I was thinking about Ted ... and you, of course.'

'I'm starting to understand what it feels like to be haunted.'

'Are there no CCTV cameras near your flat? Maybe they caught the person responsible on video?'

'I think the police are looking into it.' Slim made a mental note to check with Arthur, but in truth he didn't know. The blame had fallen at his feet for the fire, and Arthur had heard nothing about further investigation despite Slim's wishes.

'Make sure they do,' Emma said. 'Practically every square inch of this country is on camera these days.'

'I will,' he said.

Emma patted his leg. 'I don't think it's me that needs to worry. It's you. If Joanna Bramwell really is out there, perhaps she knows you're after her.'

Slim remembered the photographs. He was still yet to hear back from Arthur's friend. 'Oh, I'm sure of it,' he said.

Emma kissed him. Slim wanted to tell her to leave, to leave him to his dark thoughts and his drinking, but the part of him that needed comfort was raising its head.

He kissed her back, wishing he'd never met her, nor ever heard the names of Ted Douglas and Joanna Bramwell.

41

When he woke, the clock showed just after two. Slim rolled over, feeling for Emma, but the bed was empty. Instead, his fingers closed over a piece of paper.

The bedside lamp, when he switched it on, sent a lance of pain directly into his brain. He squinted through it to read the note, brief and to the point:

Your bed is a little small for two! I'll call you in the morning.
 And don't worry, I'll be fine.
 Emma.

Slim threw his pillow against the wall, where it hung for a moment before falling and knocking over a pot of complimentary teabags.

Emma didn't get it, that a girl practically a ghost could be capable of killing people, but then a few weeks ago he might not have either.

He sat up. Then again, had Joanna actually killed

The Man by the Sea

anyone? Not one of the dead girls had died by a human hand, despite the circumstances.

Climbing out of bed, he scrambled to the room's desk where he found a piece of paper and a pen. He was just scrawling down some notes for Arthur when he heard a voice behind him.

He spun around, his first thought that Emma was still here. She had just used the bathroom before leaving, maybe. But the bathroom light was off. Then he realised. The voice came from the closet where he had hidden his recording equipment.

Certain he had switched it off, he opened the door and found a red light blinking on the display.

The line was still active. A rustling sound came from headphones he must have unplugged. He plugged them back in and pulled them on.

'I miss you, Ted...'

Slim tried to pull the headphones off, but one cup caught on his ear, and as the hissing of the active line continued, he suppressed his immediate fear and pushed the phones back on. The voice felt so close it could have been speaking to Slim instead of Ted. It hissed, sibilant and crackly, as though rarely used.

'Can I touch you? Please?'

'No, I'm sorry. Please leave me...'

Slim scrambled for the record button, but a loud thump followed and then the sound went dead. He jumped up, throwing the headphones to the floor.

His phone was lying on the bed, but he had again forgotten to charge it. Feeling a well of anger rising up, he lifted the phone to throw it against the wall, then felt better of it and tossed it back on the bed. Instead, he grabbed his keys and headed for the door.

He needed to call Arthur, or at least Emma, but without his phone he didn't know their numbers. He cursed his incompetence, but at least he knew the way to the hospital.

He stumbled downstairs, telling himself that he was fit enough to drive, that whatever he had drunk before Emma came had been burned off by a few hours' sleep.

His car was parked up the street, halfway back to his flat. He tried to control his breathing as he walked, his old military training reminding him that panic would set his nerves tingling and make even simple actions difficult. Even so, he fumbled with the key in the lock, dropping it to the ground. He cursed as he scooped it up again, this time using his free hand to guide it.

The inside of his car seemed five degrees lower than the night outside, and momentarily the cold gave him focus. He started the engine and pulled out, quickly accelerating up to the junction with the main road.

His mind whirred with possible routes to the hospital. The more direct route passed through the centre of town, but he would have to negotiate the taxis stopping outside the clubs and groups of drunks sauntering across the street. A quicker route circuited a park but the road was single-lane width meaning he'd lose his advantage if he met another car.

His thoughts clouded with indecision. As a lorry rumbled past, he thought of Ted, lying there inert, tubes poking out of his mouth while an apparition leaned over him, one in a black trench coat and smelling of saltwater, with shell-encrusted hair and clawing hands callused from climbing cliffs. Set into a face that was a tattered remnant of beauty, dark eyes watched him over an expressionless mouth, and a hand lifted to lay a little pile of broken shells on his chest—

A horn blared. Slim spun the wheel but went right instead of left, and a collision he could have avoided happened as his front wing slammed into the rear end of a passing Ford. He jerked, the seatbelt he had remembered to use locking tight. His head lolled, and lights flashed. Metal scraped as the front car moved a short distance forward as though wanting to escape. Then it stopped, and a remaining brake light came on. The driver's door opened. A man got out and stormed back to Slim's car, still idling in the middle of the street.

As the man began to berate him through the closed window, Slim leaned back and closed his eyes.

42

The key rattled in the lock. Slim groaned, pulled back the thin blanket, and got up from the hard jail cell bed. He looked up as the door opened.

'You're free to go,' the police officer said, then frowned at Slim, as though, in reality, he would never be free again.

At the reception desk he was read the last rites of his driving life—his license was suspended with immediate effect, and while he was free to return to the burned-out remnant of his home, he would be sent a court summons within a month for a hearing most likely in December. His license would be suspended for at least a year, and a fine was a certainty. The good news—such as it was—was that as a first offense he would probably avoid jail, and an obligatory alcohol awareness course would be paid for by social services.

The police receptionist handed him a box. 'Here are your things,' she said.

'Thanks,' Slim answered, taking a shoebox with a water stain down one side that felt symbolic of his entire existence. He went outside and sat down on a step.

The Man by the Sea

He still had his phone (uncharged) and his wallet (empty besides a few coins). He was still booked into the hotel (the key not supposed to be removed had been in his pocket) but his smoke-damaged home felt like a better sanctuary, so he headed there, walking slowly, head slumped, the shoebox held in his arms as though it contained the ashes of a loved one.

He was halfway to the bus stop when a police cruiser pulled up alongside.

'Get in,' Arthur said. 'I tried to catch you but I heard they kicked you out.'

'Have you seen Ted? I asked them to call you but they said I was drunk and threw me in the cells.'

'I got a call this morning. He's fine. Well, the same. Come on, get in.'

Slim sighed and climbed in, but he had barely sat down when Arthur's fist slammed into his cheek, throwing him against the door. He turned, thinking he was in a fight, but Arthur was staring out the front, shaking his head, absently flexing the fingers on his left hand.

'I'm sorry,' he said, 'but you need to wake up. What were you playing at last night? This is very bad for you. Someone could have been killed. I can't protect you, Slim. I'll do what I can, but it's possible a magistrate could jail you. What were you thinking?'

'I had to get to Ted. She was there, I heard her.'

Arthur didn't look convinced. 'I had checks done to see if anyone was shown on the hospital's CCTV. I have a man in there, plain clothes, and he reported nothing.'

'He must have dozed off.'

'You need to stay in control. Have you been drinking yet?'

'I only woke up half an hour ago. Give me a chance.'

'Well, once we're out on the boat, you can work on keeping a clear head.'

Slim groaned. 'I forgot about that.'

Arthur rolled his eyes. 'I thought you might have.'

They drove on in silence, toward, as Slim remembered now, the harbour at Carnwell, where Arthur had rented a boat and captain to take them out to examine the cliff around the headland at Cramer Cove. Resentment radiated off Arthur like heat from a stove fire. Slim didn't need the police chief to tell him he had screwed up again. He knew it. He couldn't just accept the blame, though. The Joanna Bramwell case was gaslighting him.

'I think I'm going insane,' Slim said at last. 'And I don't think it's my fault. Let's hope we find her at last.'

'I'm looking forward to seeing the back of you both,' Arthur said, and although Slim waited for a revealing smile, none came.

The boat was waiting by the port. The captain, an ageing local fisherman, was ready to cast off. Out on the open water, to his surprise, Slim felt the kind of freedom he no longer felt on land, and the urge to pitch himself over the side into the blue-grey water became so great that he held onto the side guard rail for support.

The flat, open bay of Carnwell drifted past them and the cliffs began to steepen. Sandy beach turned into a succession of barely accessible shingle inlets, tiny semi-circles of grey between jagged cliffs.

Slim quickly lost track of where they were, and only when the captain began to slow and pointed to a beach unfolding behind a jagged promontory did he realise they had reached Cramer Cove.

'Any way you can pull us in closer to the cliff?' Arthur asked the captain.

The Man by the Sea

The old fisherman shook his head. 'No chance. You're not paying enough for a replacement boat.' He nodded at an inflatable dinghy lashed to the stern. 'You can go in on that, though. Don't drown, and don't damage it. I'll wait out here off the rocks.'

Slim looked at Arthur, who nodded.

The water was a lot choppier than it looked from the deck of the fishing boat, with the dinghy bucking about in crosswinds cutting around the promontory. Slim and Arthur rowed manfully, aiming for a break between two outcrops of rock that made a small natural harbour. At first they seemed to get nowhere, straining against a current that was intent on pushing them out to sea, then, when Slim felt his strength about to give, rocky crags began to encircle them, pulling them into the embrace of the towering cliff.

'My word, it's remote,' Arthur said. 'It would be almost impossible to get to from the beach.'

'Except for an experienced climber,' Slim said, remembering Andrea Clark, who had died out here on these rocks. 'It's pretty treacherous, though.'

'A good place to hide. Let's go take a look.'

Slim had done some river training in the army, but that was over twenty years ago. Still, he had more experience than Arthur, so he climbed out first as they steered the dinghy up onto a flat lip of rock. He held it steady as Arthur started to climb out, then as the police chief caught an outcrop of rock with his hands and started to loop his leg over, Slim gave the dinghy a shove. Arthur slipped, one leg going into the water, soaking him up to the waist. As he cried out, Slim grabbed his arm and pulled him up.

Slim offered Arthur a smile. 'That's for punching me.'

'You reckless bastard.'

Slim shrugged. 'I haven't had a drink yet today. I'm tense. Though I appreciated the pep talk. I'll bear it in mind.'

Arthur scowled, but allowed Slim to help him up onto the rocks.

They pulled the dinghy out of the water and lodged it into a crevasse. Then they began clambering over rocks, looking for some sign that a person had been here.

'By my best estimation, that ladder should be somewhere above us,' Arthur said.

The lower part of the cliff was jagged but climbable for someone with guts or experience, but from about halfway, the cliff turned almost sheer, a wall of treacherous shale ledges and outcrops. A slight angle left the top out of sight, and Slim peered up, trying to spot any sign of ladders or chains.

'No caves or anything,' Arthur said. 'I mean, there are a few slight overhangs, but nothing someone could live inside. I guess it's possible she was launching a boat from down here, but if that's the case she could be anywhere. We'd have to search the whole coast.'

Slim nodded. 'That ladder went somewhere. Perhaps she climbs down and then swims for the beach.'

They continued to look around for a while, climbing around the cliff as far as they were able without getting back into the water, but they could find no other trace of Joanna Bramwell. Frustrated, Slim squatted down by the water's edge and watched the way it sucked and shoved against the cliff's outcrops. There was something, just out of reach. He frowned wishing he were drunk, that the offbeat viewpoints a little liquor gave him were here to spark his imagination.

A horn blared.

The Man by the Sea

'That's the captain,' Arthur said. 'I think we've overstayed our welcome.'

'I'm thinking,' Slim said. 'Just a minute.'

The horn blared again.

'Do you want him to leave us here?'

Reluctantly Slim followed Arthur back to where they had left the dinghy.

Back on the boat, the captain informed them that the radio had warned of a turn in the weather, which, coupled with the rising tide, meant that within an hour it might be impossible to get off the rocks. Slim glared at what was still a calm sea, angry to be denied when he felt sure they had been close to a breakthrough.

By the time they were back at the docks, clouds had rolled in and waves were slapping at the shore. Arthur drove Slim home to Yatton in pouring rain, but when Slim walked into the hotel, the manager was waiting to meet him.

'Mr. Hardy?

Slim felt as though he had jumped into the frothing seas off Cramer Cove. 'Yes?'

'I'm very sorry to have to tell you this, but your credit card has been rejected. We have to ask you to leave.'

43

The lights in his flat didn't work, but he found a plug low on one wall with a current, so he could at least charge his phone. Then, using an extension cord, he took a lamp from the bedroom and sat at the fire-damaged dining table to survey the wreckage of his life.

His laptop wouldn't work, but even if it would, the flash-drive on which he kept his data had been taken by the ghost who started the fire. He couldn't cook because his cooker was blown, and the single plug wouldn't handle the wattage of the microwave.

His fridge had defrosted, his wallet was empty, and his last bottle of whisky was also empty.

It felt like the end of the world.

Joanna Bramwell had done a fine job of destroying the evidence he had assembled. He had little hope for his laptop, which had suffered both fire and water damage, while the box of papers Emma had provided—which had conveniently moved itself beside the cooker—was a heap of ash.

He was just thinking to perhaps get a paperback from

The Man by the Sea

the shelf and embrace a little escapism when the single plug sparked and the light went out.

He caught the last bus from Yatton back to Carnwell, waiting until he had walked within a couple of streets before he called Emma.

She didn't sound convinced by his explanation that he was worried about her safety with Ted still in hospital, but she told him to come around the back, out of view of the police officer already watching her house.

'I'm not sure this is a good idea,' she said, letting him in, then quickly shutting the door. She led him through into a rear living room which already had the curtains drawn. A newspaper was laid out neatly on a dining table of sheet glass covering an ancient-style sepia world map-designed cloth. Full but tidy shelves filled one wall, a neatly-ordered bookcase another. Curtains hung to a single inch above a polished mantel. The carpet, in contrast to the intricacies seen elsewhere, was a plain dark red.

'Tea? I'm afraid I don't have anything stronger.'

Slim grimaced. He could do it. Easy. He didn't drink so much anyway.

'Sure,' he said, hoping his unease wasn't evident.

'I'm afraid I haven't cleaned,' she said, when it looked like cleaning was all she did.

'Don't worry. I apologise for the suddenness of my visit. I'm not quite houseless, but I'm certainly lacking a decent quality home.'

'It won't look good,' she said. 'You over here, staying the night with me, while my husband's in a hospital bed. You are staying the night, aren't you?'

Slim shrugged. 'I guess, if it's offered.'

Emma smiled. 'You know it is.'

He let what he expected to happen, happen. It wasn't

easy; he was hungry, both for food and drink. But Emma was hungry too, and took from him what she wanted.

Around midnight he awoke. Emma was snoring heavily beside him, but she had left a small nightlight on which cast the bedroom with a spectral glow. Slim, his hands trembling from a need he couldn't deny much longer, got up, knowing there would be no more sleep until his cravings were satisfied.

The bedroom was as neat as the living room downstairs. Something seemed odd that it took Slim, in his increasingly agitated state, a moment to realise, was that this was an entirely woman's room: the bed a queen rather than king, suitable for sex but less so for two sleepers side by side, while the dressers and drawers and a dressing table showed no sign that a man had ever entered this room before him.

So where did Ted sleep?

Slim crept to the window and pulled back the curtain a crack. It looked down onto a back lawn that ended in a tall fence bordering a small park. The park had two entrances, and the plain-clothed police officer was positioned to view both. Slim, aware of the man's presence, had taken great pains to climb over a chain link fence in the shadow of a stand of trees to gain access to Emma's garden unnoticed, but if Joanna Bramwell was out there somewhere, it would be hard to get close to the house without alerting someone to her presence.

Slim squinted. Was she out there now, watching? Or had she returned to the hospital to torment Ted?

Emma was still snoring. Slim went out into a hall and closed the door quietly. Three doors led off. The first was a bathroom, the second a sparse guest bedroom. The third was a man's room.

The Man by the Sea

Slim slipped inside, closed the door, and then pushed the curtains wide to allow the faint glow from the streetlights to enter. The window looked out on the street, and he saw the same car outside, the police officer maintaining his vigil. He squatted down and waited for his eyes to adjust.

The room was far sparser than Emma's, but a bookshelf of action thrillers and a few books on fly fishing that looked rarely touched identified it as where Ted slept. The bed was neatly made, the duvet unblemished, a single teddy bear nestled in against the pillow. While Slim appreciated that in modern times it wasn't unusual for married couples to sleep apart, it was an indication of the decline in the Douglas's marriage that the separate room situation was so embedded.

He also recognised the fortune of information his own misfortune had granted him. By the light of the streetlights, he began to search.

Soon his shakes had gotten so bad that he was thinking to go in search of a 24-hour supermarket, his frustration getting the better of him. He struggled to replace unfolded clothes and old work documents in Ted's perfectly sanitised man-space. Everything was so mundane that Slim wondered if he'd been mistaken all along. The Ted from the beach couldn't be the Ted who lived a mannequin's life of uniformity.

By the time his bowels began to play up, Slim was ready to tell Emma he was done, that it was time for him to walk away. He sat on the toilet, harbouring a growing resentment toward Ted and Joanna for so thoroughly covering their tracks. He wished he could flush them away, too.

The cabinet above the sink was ajar, and inside, Slim

found a bottle of mouthwash. It was a poor man's pick up, but it was something. He took a long swallow, then topped up the level from the tap so Emma wouldn't notice.

As he was about to head for bed, he paused. He flushed the toilet again, frowning. There was something about the way the water swirled in the pipe that got him thinking.

44

'Are you going to tell me what this is about?'

Slim couldn't keep the grin off his face as the sea wind rustled off his hair.

'Of course, it wouldn't be simple,' he said. 'Nothing is with Joanna Bramwell. Why would this be any different?'

'You're not making any sense.'

'I'll explain when we arrive.'

Despite the captain's reluctance, they paddled onto the rocks in far choppier waters than before. The tide was slurping and sucking at crags and gullies as they lodged the dinghy.

'Right there,' Slim said, clambering over a jagged ridge onto a ledge extending out into the water. 'See the way the chop comes in here but doesn't splash up over the rocks? That's because it's not meeting the same resistance. There's something down there.'

'What?'

Slim pulled off his shirt and unzipped the holdall he had brought. The ragged wetsuit had cost him his last few quid in Carnwell's Oxfam shop, and it tore a little as he pulled it on. Before he zipped it up, he stuffed a sealable plastic bag containing a torch and an old camera Arthur had lent him inside the suit, nestled it against his stomach, then zipped it up again.

'Slim, we have police divers,' Arthur said. 'At the very least I could have got you some decent gear. You don't even have a face mask. This is—'

'Reckless?' Slim grinned. He held up shaking hands. 'I've had one drink in twenty-four hours, and that tasted of spearmint. I spent the morning vomiting in Tesco's' public toilet. Right now, cracking my head on those rocks doesn't sound so bad.'

'Your suit's on backward,' Arthur said. 'The zip should be at the back.'

Slim grinned. 'Wish me luck.'

'Good luck, you crazy fool.'

Slim looked down into the water. The sea, sucking and pulling at the rocks, was doing so with frightening force. It was likely to smash him like a rotten apple against a wall.

Taking what he hoped wasn't his last breath, he shut his eyes and jumped.

Even with the wetsuit, the shock of the cold was staggering. He gasped, losing the precious breath he had saved, and then he was under, freezing, salty water wrapping around him.

With currents tugging him, he had no control of direction. Aware of the shelf of rock on which Arthur stood above, he flapped his hands to push downward, letting the momentum of the water drive his progress. It sucked, pulling him out, then with a roar it flung him forward at what should have been a wall of jagged rock.

Slim waited to die, but where he should have met cold, bone-crushing resistance, there was nothing. Face down,

The Man by the Sea

his back scrapped at something above, and his hands found rock beneath. The water surged, pushing him forward again, and he burst out of the water, arching his neck at the same time to take in a desperate breath.

He was in darkness.

The rock beneath his hands was smooth and slick. Water still sucked at his feet, so he scrambled forward, and wet rocks became dry and rough, and then he felt pebbles and shale under his fingers. With the sound of the water behind him, Slim rolled over and sat up. He sat quietly, his eyes closed, listening to the hollow echo of the sea battering the headland, and the wind whistling around the cliff.

When he opened his eyes, he saw a thin shaft of light.

Water dripped from the end of a natural borehole in the ceiling onto a patch of rock gleaming in the sun. Slim looked up the shaft, barely wide enough for a person to enter. Rocks had been piled beneath it to provide a way up to where hand- and footholds chipped into its sides gave access to the cliff face some ten or fifteen metres above.

'That's how you get in and out,' he whispered, his voice echoing back at him from the damp cave walls.

He pulled off the top half of his wetsuit, noticing the warmth of the cave compared to the air outside.

The torchlight illuminated a cavern stretching some way past the borehole, an accumulation of rock debris gradually rising up to meet the sloping cave roof.

As the light fell over a flat area cleared of stones, Slim stopped and stared.

Around him, stacked up against the rock walls, was a life: a miscellany of accumulated items, everything from foodstuffs to books, threadbare blankets, plastic chairs, bottles and cans, old torches, a heap of rusted batteries, gas canisters and even some electrical items that may never have worked.

Slim picked a dog-eared paperback out of a plastic box and turned it over.

Romeo and Juliet.

As he opened it to a bookmarked page, the folded piece of paper fell out.

He picked it up and turned it over in his hands.

A flyer for a Shakespeare company. On the front, in all their headline splendour, Ted Douglas and Joanna Bramwell.

Slim replaced the bookmark and put the book back into the box. A strange feeling came over him, one that blended euphoria with a bittersweet regret.

'I've found you,' he whispered. 'At last.'

45

'You're a madman,' Arthur said, shaking his head. 'But if you want a job on Carnwell's police force, say the word. I'll find some way to fast-track you. You're wasted spying on dirty old men.'

Slim smiled. His face still ached from where he had struck his cheek during the arduous climb out. At the time seemingly a good idea, in hindsight it would have been less dangerous to risk the underwater tunnel a second time, but by the time he had scrambled to the top of the borehole on cut and bleeding feet, only to find himself facing fifty metres of near-vertical rock face with only a few rusty chains and ladders to help him, going back was as dangerous as going forward.

From the clifftop he had hurried to the beach, where he had been able to attract the attention of the boat's captain. The bemused fisherman had let Arthur know, and then come in close enough to the beach for Slim to swim out. Back on the boat, Arthur had stared at Slim as though he were Joanna Bramwell herself.

'Where the hell did you get to?' he exclaimed, shaking

his head. 'I was about to call out the coastguard to look for a body.'

Slim smiled. 'I'm not sure you're going to believe this.'

The photos Slim had taken were proof enough of Joanna Bramwell's secret den. Arthur flicked through them, shaking his head in disbelief.

'How on earth did she find that place?' he said.

'She didn't. It found her. After a streak of bad luck, Joanna got some fortune. It's my belief that after your friend Mick threw her body into the sea, the water washed her into the cave. There she woke up, born again.'

'It sounds like you've been reading a bunch of that Shakespeare, too,' Arthur said.

'I have no other explanation, but it fits. And how else can you explain such a place? My guess it was a cave used by smugglers—hence the chains and ladders. Perhaps it was a local legend? I don't know.'

'I've never heard anything,' Arthur said. 'But it was so well hidden I can believe you're right. It's invisible from both the sea and the clifftop.'

'A perfect hiding place,' Slim said. 'Now we just have to find her. I don't think it's the only place she hides out. There was no fresh food, nothing to suggest she had been there in some time.'

'Another cave?'

Slim shrugged. 'I think it's unlikely. It might be time you called in a full police manhunt.'

Arthur looked pained. 'I tried. I don't have the authorisation. There's still not enough to go on.'

Slim clenched his fists. 'There's a dangerous woman out there.'

Arthur shook his head. 'Here's what it came down to with my superiors. All the cases involved have been

The Man by the Sea

officially solved. And even if they weren't, there was nothing to say they were murder. Unfortunately fear isn't a murderer's weapon.'

'Then we have to find her ourselves,' Slim said. 'Listen, this is going to make me sound bad, but I need some cash.'

'For drink? Slim, if you're that desperate, I can clean out my liquor cabinet—'

'Food, bus tickets, and I need to fix up some gear that got broken.' He grinned. 'But if you did, that would be grand.'

'I can't just hand over a wad of notes.'

'I'll pay you back. I just need a sub for a couple of weeks.'

Arthur rolled his eyes. 'I'll do what I can.'

'And I need CCTV footage. My street, the Douglas's street, the approach to the hospital.'

'I told you, I can't authorise that level of manpower—'

'Then I'll watch it all myself. I have nothing better to do. And those photos I gave you—do you have them back yet?'

'I've heard nothing.'

'Chase them up. Supposing there's a clue in all that getup. Anything you can do, I need. It's important.'

'What are you going to do?'

Slim gritted his teeth. 'I'm going to find Joanna Bramwell ... even if it kills me.'

46

Slim was beginning to understand how Ted Douglas must have felt. He had never been haunted before, but he awoke to Emma's snoring with a sheen of sweat across his back and a residue terror of being held underwater by a woman's skeletal hands.

He pulled back the sheets and crawled to the door. The door to Ted's room was slightly ajar, so he crept inside, beginning another silent search through drawers and cupboards. Again, nothing. Emma had said the box of papers had come from the loft, so perhaps he would have better luck there. It was impossible to access without waking Emma, though. Perhaps he could convince her to visit Ted in hospital, leaving him at the house … he didn't think so.

He sat back against Ted's bed, feeling frustrated. Answers were waiting for him, but where?

A creak came from the hallway. Slim started to get up, but too late, a light came on in the hall and then Ted's door was opening. Emma stood there in her nightgown, rubbing her eyes. With her hair ruffled, and without the benefit of makeup, she had gained ten years.

'What are you doing in here?'

Slim started to make an excuse, but gave up. He sighed.

'I'm looking for clues,' he said.

For a few seconds he thought Emma would explode with anger at this intrusion into her privacy, but she just cocked her head at him like a tired parent, then sat on the floor beside him.

'If there was anything to find, don't you think I would have brought it to you?'

'I thought you might have missed something.'

'Believe me, all this business with Ted and Joanna was a surprise to me, too. I'll admit our marriage wasn't doing great—you can see that—but it was a marriage. Have you come up with nothing?'

Slim thought about telling Emma about the cave, but he didn't want to get her hopes up. Instead, he said, 'I'm trying to get hold of some CCTV footage.'

Emma nodded. 'That might help. I hope you catch her soon. Shall we go back to bed?'

Slim nodded. As they reached the hall, he nodded at the bathroom. 'Just a minute.'

Emma smiled. 'I'll be waiting.'

They parted. Slim, his stomach churning as it had the previous night, squatted on the toilet and waited. Emma's bedroom door clicked shut.

When he was done, he went to wash his hands, but found the shaking worse than it had been in several days. He tried to hold his hands still enough to turn off the faucet, but it was no use. He nudged open the sink cabinet and reached for the mouthwash. It was better than nothing and would last him until to the morning.

His fingers knocked it backward. The plastic wall at the cabinet's back came loose. Slim grimaced, afraid it would fall into the space behind, but it had lodged tight. He tried to pull it out to realign it, but it was meeting resistance from something pressed in behind.

Perhaps it had fallen out before. Slim tried to twist it back into place, but it lifted up, and he saw the corner of something paper poking out.

A notebook.

After a long swallow of mouthwash steadied his hands, Slim removed the other items from the cabinet and then slid out the plastic rear wall.

An old pencil-lined notebook stood in the space behind, perched on a lip of plastic, leaning against an unpainted section of wall.

Slim removed it and opened it to the first page.

'I can't believe I found you,' he read. *'I've always wanted to tell you I was sorry.'*

With hands shaking worse than before, Slim slid the notebook back where it had been resting, then replaced the plastic wall and the other items in the cabinet.

When he climbed in next to Emma, she rolled over, waking from a half-sleep, and groaned.

'You took your time,' she said.

'My stomach's playing up,' Slim answered. 'Sorry.'

47

I THOUGHT MY EYES WERE DECEIVING ME. I MOURNED YOU, Joanna, and I suffered for what I did to you. For years I was dead inside. Even when I coached myself back into life through the simple need to exist, a part of me was missing. A part of me that died with you on that beach.

I went to your funeral. I held my tears while others around me made rivers of theirs. Outwardly, I was a stone wall of respect, but behind the stoicism of my face, I was dying, too, throttled inside with the twin garrottes of guilt and loss. You know, don't you, that I made a mistake? I was selfish. I wanted you all for myself.

I'm sorry, Joanna. I will never forgive myself for what I did, and I do not deserve your forgiveness. Yet, when you looked into my eyes, I felt it there.

I don't know what brought me to return to Cramer Cove that day I found you again. I guess I was hunting for ghosts, still haunted by the look in your eyes that last day, when you told me that our feelings didn't matter, that you had made a choice. I wanted only to walk by the sea and think of you, but when I found you there, standing by the shoreline, I felt that I had also died and that our spirits would walk together forevermore.

I almost let you be. I almost waited by my car until your apparition faded, but I felt a stirring inside that had been missing since the days we were together.

'Joanna.'

It was the first time I had spoken your name aloud in nearly ten years. From the way your shoulders shifted I knew you had heard me, and when you turned, the joy that flooded through me buckled my knees. I looked on your face for the first time in years from below you. The sun framed your hair, and I felt like I had been thrown back in time.

As your eyes looked over me, I prayed that you would utter my name. I wanted to beg you, but you were already leaving me, returning to the water. You belonged to the sea now, I realised, a Shakespearean heroine brought to life. I watched you disappear, the water rising around you, and I cried for what had been found as well as what had been lost.

There was little in life that has hurt me more than to turn from you and return to my now world, one in which you no longer exist.

I will return for you, Joanna. I will never leave you again.

48

'He led a secret life,' Slim told Arthur over a coffee he had laced with a cheap no-brand whisky. Already half of Arthur's quiet sub was gone on what Slim considered essentials—three cheap bottles of booze, a second-hand microwave and a stack of packet meals to go with it, and a four-week bus pass.

Arthur shook his head. 'But there are no clues to where Joanna might be?'

'None. He writes with what I'd consider a suppressed poeticism. Like this notebook is his outlet for everything that died in him when Joanna did. Some of it's written in verse. It's barely legible.'

'Can I see it?'

Slim shook his head. 'I left it in the house. The wall of the cabinet had been warped over time because of the notebook and wouldn't fit back in without the notebook behind it. My guess is that Ted has been stashing it there for decades. I had to put it back.'

'Couldn't you find something to replace it?'

Slim grinned. 'I'm heading down to WH Smiths when we're done here.'

'Didn't you want Emma to see? It might have offered her closure.'

Slim shook his head. 'She's not the forgiving type, and I'm worried about how she might react to finding out her husband was effectively cheating on her with a ghost.'

Arthur rubbed his eyes, then gave Slim a stern look. 'You know, it does complicate matters that you're sleeping with her.'

When Slim feigned surprise, Arthur shook his head.

'You think I haven't noticed?' He shrugged. 'To be honest, I wasn't sure until now. You're not a good liar.'

Slim shrugged. 'It just kind of happened. I wasn't preying on a woman in distress or anything like that.'

'You're putting yourself in the firing line.'

Slim nodded. 'I'm also close to the action if Joanna shows up. I wanted to end it—'

'—before it ends you?'

Slim gave a wry smile. 'Something like that.'

Arthur shrugged. 'I hope you know what you're doing.' He leaned over and hauled a plastic bag up onto the table. Items jostled inside. 'Keep the door locked behind you while you're trawling through these.'

Slim lifted the edge of the bag and peered inside. 'What's this?'

'CCTV tapes.'

Slim withdrew a VHS tape and lifted it up. 'Actual video tapes? I'm not sure I have anything to play these on.'

'There's a mixture. Depends on how old the system was. I've labelled each location.'

Slim grinned. 'Should make a good date night with Emma. Popcorn's in the bag, right?'

The Man by the Sea

Arthur ignored the sarcasm. 'I'm allocating as many officers I can to this,' Arthur said. 'I'm doubling street patrols. I justified it as a precaution against the usual pre-Christmas crime you always get at this time of year, but they've all been briefed with Joanna's description.'

'Water-soaked, matted, shell-encrusted hair, dressed in a fisherman's trench-coat and waders? You sure they took you seriously?'

'I toned it down a little from the description you gave me. Made her sound like a vagabond, long-term homeless.'

'Good call.'

Slim stood up. 'I'll be in touch.'

'Good luck.'

They shook hands then went their separate ways.

Slim was buzzing both inside and out. He had his tasks to do, but all he could think about was getting back to Emma's and secreting the time to chart his way through Ted's ornate, tightly written script. He had read only a few pages the night before, most of which had been stream-of-conscious meanderings rather than hard facts, but it was already clear that Ted was unsure whether he found himself interacting with a real person or a ghost, or something in between.

49

It became the focus of my existence. Hiding my reasons from Emma, I took every opportunity to return to Carnwell and search for you. I know that early on, she suspected nothing, but as time went on, I believe her suspicions were aroused. What could I tell her? That I had found you after all these years?

The truth was, I didn't find you. As business and a variety of obscure reasons brought me home, I had just that solitary meeting upon which to rest all of my hopes. I searched, but it was eight long years before I caught another glimpse of the apparition you had become.

Of course, by then you had become a figment of local folklore, and perhaps I was partly responsible for an image of a woman born of the sea to assume your name. Men with loose tongues in late-night bars will pass information better than newspapers will. Yet, that I was not alone in seeing this apparition gave me hope that—some part of you, at least—still existed.

I dreamed of a true reuniting, of the chance to make amends, and perhaps to forge a life with you that was never mine to have. I dreamed, Joanna. I'm sorry, but I dreamed.

And then I heard about the dead girl, and the world I was beginning to understand flipped on its head.

50

The electricity had been repaired, and a lucky break with the credit card company had given Slim enough to pay for it. A cheap VHS recorder he had bought in a charity shop stood on a stack of water-damaged cookbooks Slim had never used, making a worrying clicking sound as it played a grainy video of the street outside Emma Douglas's house.

Slim, pressing a whisky glass against his eyes to hold them open, did as Arthur had suggested, fast-forwarding through the quiet hours when not even a car passing was visible on the triangle of street caught in the view-finder from a neighbour's security camera five doors down from Ted's house, waiting for people, then pausing, rewinding, reviewing, moving on.

The way to overcome the boredom was to segment it, Arthur had told him. One thing at a time. Focus on the people, eliminate them, then deal with the vehicles.

Military sentry duty had taught him the need for patience, but late at night, already drunk, eyes sore from trying to focus on bad quality images, it wasn't easy.

He checked the timer on the video, found it to be a good hour after the fire in the Douglas's car, then withdrew it and tossed it onto a pile of discarded tapes. Or was that the maybes pile? Slim rubbed his eyes, struggling to remember.

The nearest tape to hand was from the security camera of a hairdresser three doors down from his flat, the only one on his street.

With a sigh, Slim slid it into the machine. According to Arthur, the camera had been vandalised on the same night of the fire at Slim's flat. The view finder showed a section of pavement with the high street behind. A tree to the left cast a shadow left by a streetlight just behind it.

Every few seconds, the camera shook lightly. Slim looked for passing cars causing the lens to shake, then a flurry of movement obscuring the view told him everything he needed to know.

A bird was nesting on top of the camera.

Slim, an early hangover starting to grow as the view continued to shake at regular intervals, squinted as the minutes ticked past. There seemed little point continuing to watch; besides the occasional car, there was little of interest. The few people who had walked past had all gone in the opposite direction.

He was about to switch off and turn in for the night when a figure stepped into view.

Thick braids of black hair pushed out at a hood that covered the face beneath, deepening the shadow already left by the tree.

Joanna Bramwell.

Terror broke through Slim's stupor, and he reached for the remote to switch off his television. At the last moment

The Man by the Sea

he stopped, transfixed as Joanna lifted a hand that began to wave like a pendulum from side to side.

'You're mocking me, damn you,' Slim muttered.

As her waving continued, Slim, his courage slowly eking back, leaning forward, wishing he could see beneath that black hood.

He was just inches from the screen when Joanna Bramwell jerked forward, and the screen went black.

A scream died in Slim's throat. As the view turn to static, he reached for his bottle.

51

DROWNED.

I told myself it was impossible you were involved, and even when the inquest concluded, there was not enough evidence to suggest otherwise.

Becca Lees was nine and by all accounts couldn't even swim. Did you see her? Did you see anything?

I know that what I did tied you to Cramer Cove in a way it's hard to understand, but I remember you, Joanna. I remember your smile. You would never have hurt anyone. You had the sweetest soul. Perhaps my mistake changed you, or perhaps I've been mistaken.

All I saw was an apparition, after all.

52

'She knew,' Slim said. 'She knew someone would see her.'

Arthur leaned over the laptop and replayed the converted video clip for what felt to Slim like the hundredth time.

'It won't change,' Slim said. 'She knew where to stand to ensure her face would be hidden.'

'We've got a good lock on her clothes, at least,' Arthur said. 'I'll distribute updated descriptions to my officers. The net's closing, Slim. We'll have her within days, I'm sure of it.'

'No, you won't.'

'What?'

'Look at her. She's avoided every other camera except the only one where we couldn't get a clear look at her. And there she taunts us.'

'She was knocking off the bird's nest. She must have something against them.'

'No. That's just a cover. We're being duped. Joanna Bramwell is cold and calculating, and she's one step ahead of us. She knows we're trailing her, but she's playing us for fools.'

'I'll double the officers on the streets.'

'It won't make a difference. We have to get ahead of her.'

'Ted?'

'I think if she planned to kill him, he would already be dead.'

Arthur rubbed his eyes. 'We're hunting someone who's likely brain-damaged, prone to violence, and prefers solitude. How can she hide out in plain sight? Look at her. She's a walking caricature.'

Arthur made to turn the laptop around, but Slim put up a hand. 'I've seen enough,' he said. 'We've got to get ahead of her.'

'I'm out of ideas.'

Slim sighed. 'Me, too.'

53

It was a stupid idea, but Slim couldn't resist. Carnwell Royal Infirmary was an unassuming series of three-storey buildings set in a half-hearted attempt at landscape gardens at the top of Carnwell's only real hill. The view from the bus stop was one of a quiet, grey town laid out in a rough semi-circle around the curve of a sandy bay. Small fishing boats lay on the sand, while larger commercial vessels clustered around a dredged harbour at the end of a breakwater. North and south the land rose, northward beginning an undulation that would flatten out again at Morecombe Bay, south on the march to Wales, passing the rugged cliffs of Cramer Cove.

It was pretty, lacking the dramatics of Scotland or Cornwall, but a pleasant place to live, one that didn't deserve to be haunted by a wraith from the sea who ought to be dead.

Slim signed in as a friend of Ted's, but was required to show ID for police checks, meaning that by tomorrow Arthur would know what he had done. If he were honest with himself, he had expected to be turned away, but with an orderly muttering about how few visitors Ted had received, Slim allowed himself to be led down a clinical if weathered corridor into the hospital's heart.

A man with the hard eyes of a plain-clothes police officer was strolling up and down the second floor corridor where the orderly indicated Ted's room. On a chair outside, a copy of the *Daily Telegraph* lay open on the racing news. Slim waited while the orderly hurried off to confer with the police officer, who nodded, then waved a nonchalant hand toward Ted's door as though he considered this whole exercise a waste of police money and time.

The orderly reiterated what Slim had already figured out, then held the door for Slim to slip inside.

Ted Douglas lay on the room's only bed, turned to face the window with its view inland toward the Pennines, as though the rugged hills rising in the distance might encourage him to awaken. His eyes were closed, and pipes snaked out of his mouth and nose, linking him to a machine that hummed alongside. His breathing was shallow, long drawn-out breaths, his chest rising and falling in a hypnotic rhythm.

Slim pulled a plastic chair away from the wall and sat down. The room was depressingly empty, Ted's only companion a pile of generic thrillers with library stickers on their spines. Otherwise, the room lacked even a token vase of flowers.

'Well, Ted, we meet at last,' Slim said, feeling both strange to speak aloud, and that it was the only appropriate way to treat a man whom he knew well, even though Ted knew nothing about him. 'I have to say, I actually feel like we're friends of a sort. We have a connection, that's for sure. Joanna Bramwell is screwing me almost as badly as she screwed you. Did she sit in this very same chair? Or did she just stand?'

Yet, even as the questions left his lips, Slim felt a sense of the absurd, like a crowd of clowns hiding behind a curtain, covering their mouths as they laughed at him.

As though he were being duped.

A creeping sense of unease overcame him, and he turned to glance back at the door.

Closed, no one peering through the little window, no one hiding in a dark corner, crouching in a gap between the machines, a bleached-white smile just too wide to be sane—

Slim stood up sharply, and paced around the bed. He pulled the hip flask from his pocket and took a long swallow, scowling when it ran empty.

'I know you loved her,' he said, feeling a need to fill the uneasy quiet. 'You wanted to be with her but you were a goddamn stargazer, weren't you? All you had to do was tell her to her face. And if she laughed at you ... you wouldn't be the first.'

He spun on his heels, eyes scanning every corner of the room, searching for what it was that had shredded his nerves.

'People have died, Ted. People have died because of that crazy bitch. They've died because you couldn't let her live her life. Why did you do it, Ted? Goddamn it, tell me.'

He was on his knees, unsure how he had got there, his hands on the edge of the bed, staring at Ted's grey face, the closed eyes, the tubes protruding from Ted's mouth, and he was back there again, smoke rising from the sand, staring at a pair of boots.

'Sir? Are you all right, sir?'

Slim looked up. The policeman stood over him, one

hand on his shoulder, firm enough to suggest comfort could turn to restraint if Slim became difficult.

'What?' Slim pushed himself up. 'I'm sorry. It's just … seeing him like this … it's not easy.'

'Visiting time is over, I'm afraid. You can come back again tomorrow.' The policeman gave an apologetic nod in Ted's direction. 'I'm afraid there's not likely to be much change in his condition.'

'Stop saying that.'

'Saying what?'

Slim turned on the policeman, who took a step back. Slim had never felt imposing, but his frame still held some of the years of military training, enough, at least, to unnerve this small town policeman.

'Stop saying you're afraid. You're not. You don't know what afraid means. Do you know how it really feels to not sleep at night? To be too afraid to close your eyes?'

'Sir … I think you need to leave.'

'I'm going, I'm going.' Slim backed away toward the door. He took one last look around, and finally understood the feeling that had come over him.

He wasn't looking for something that was out of place.

He was looking for something that should have been, but was not.

54

'Where are you, Joanna?'

Slim threw the empty hip flask at the wall of a local bank. It clattered away with a rattle and came to rest in a gutter. Slim swung a kick at it as he passed, but he missed and almost overbalanced. Scowling, he moved on up the high street.

Word must have got out fast, because there were three missed calls on his phone from Arthur, but the police chief had been unable to leave a message because Slim's memory was full. He didn't need to hear the police chief's words, because he knew them already.

Failed. Failed. Failed.

Joanna Bramwell was a ghost after all, unable to be constrained by cuffs or chains, her cage the fragility of Slim's eroding confidence. He was out of his depth, floundering in rips more powerful than those of Cramer Cove, and would soon be dragged under.

He forgot time as he wandered the streets, angry and hateful, wishing Emma Douglas had called someone else and left him alone.

Boots in the sand.

An underwater cave.

A face peering up at a video screen, unheard, unseen laughter mocking him like the chattering of carrion crows.

The taxi ride was a blur. The road where the taxi's meter reached the limit of his money dark and unforgiving. The walk down to the beach a stumbling affair of knocked ankles and scuffed shoes.

Waves battered the shore, the remnants of an Irish Sea storm. Slim walked to the waterline, stopping only when the remnants of far off breakers sloshed over his shoes.

He stared out into the night, the only light coming from occasional glimpses of the moon through cloud. Rain beat down, slashing at his face like the ocean's claws, and he felt his knees land in waterlogged sand.

He didn't know if he was crying. The only boots in the sand were his, the rest of his body gone far away.

'Are you there?' he called into the night. 'Ted couldn't banish you, could he? No matter how hard he tried. Answer me, Joanna.'

Weariness was like god sticking two fingers under his ribs. Slim closed his eyes and slumped forward onto the sand.

55

I tried to forget you. Believe me, I tried. Every time I drove south, back to my job and my home and my wife, I tried to put you to the back of my mind.

I throw myself into my work, filling my head with numbers to drown out the words that haunt every waking hour. Yet, something always comes up—a work trip, a sick friend, a family affair—that brings me back. I cannot escape you. You and I are attached by a string, Joanna, one that cannot be severed.

Yours is a name spoken in dark corners, behind closed doors. Three people dead, and no one will face the truth. It destroys me to think you might be involved, or god forbid, responsible. I will come back for good one day, I promise, and I will put an end to this. You have my word. If it's you that needs to be freed, I will free you. And if it's the rest of Carnwell, then by heaven, I'll free them, too.

56

There could be no better time for such exhilaration than when death felt so welcome. Slim's forehead contained a marching band as he climbed to the edge of the cliff and lowered himself toward the first jutting ladder. Heart thundering, he felt with his feet, finding purchase. With no other choice, he lifted his feet again, then pushed his body into a slide. At the moment he began to accelerate, he felt metal against his forearm and clutched desperately at a rung of the ladder gummed up with scree and patches of grass. Below his flailing feet, waves crashed and spray burst up over an outcrop of rocks that waited to slay him should he fall. He gave the nightmarish drop one glance then decided it was best not to look again.

The climb down was far harder than the climb up had been. He had to negotiate treacherous gaps and ledges between the ropes and chains by going feet first. When he reached the borehole—itself deep enough to be fatal if he fell—it felt like a saviour.

He was bleeding from a dozen cuts by the time his

The Man by the Sea

descent was over. The light from the morning sun cast the insides of the cave in a spectral glow, and Slim, exhausted, sat down hard on shingle untouched by water for countless years.

'It's been a long road, Joanna,' he said. 'I'm tired now. No more boots in the sand, is that okay by you? I'm done with all that. Done and dusted.'

The cave gave no answer. Slim sat still for a while then stood and went over to the ramshackle bookcase.

The copy of *Romeo and Juliet* lay where he had left it. He took it back to the shaft of light and withdrew the makeshift bookmark.

A tear ran down the side of his face as he looked at the faded line of actors with Ted and Joanna in the centre. Then, he turned the paper over and read the list of names.

'I wouldn't make much of a detective, would I?' he muttered, giving a little laugh. 'I don't think I'll be taking that job, after all.'

He carefully folded up the sheet of paper and replaced it into the book.

'Now, where are you? You've been here all along, haven't you?'

He went back to the bookcase and pulled it away from the cave wall. Ancient wood creaked as it began to break up, salty air having first made it brittle and then fragile. At first, the dark space behind kept its secrets, but as Slim's eyes began to adjust, there appeared the shape of a woman lying on her side, knees pulled up, one hand resting beneath her face, the other lying across her chest.

Slim reached down and touched fingers as dry and brittle as the squid pods that were left on the high tide line to bake in the sun.

'Oh, Joanna,' he whispered. 'How long have you been down here? Ten, twenty years?'

Joanna Bramwell's long-dead corpse gave no answer.

57

'I wondered when you'd show up,' Emma said. 'I cooked for you last night. It went cold, but it's in the fridge. You can heat it if you want it.'

Slim smiled. 'Thanks. Maybe later.'

Emma went through into the kitchen. Slim followed. Two cups sat upturned in the drying rack. Another pair of glass tumblers sat on a polished marble worktop, filled to halfway with an amber liquid.

'Well, I thought you might like a drink.'

Slim stared for a long time at the glasses, then shook his head.

'I'll pass.'

Emma shrugged. 'Suit yourself. I won't.' She scooped up the nearest glass and downed it in a single swallow. She suppressed a cough with the back of her hand, touched her lips with two fingers then glared at Slim, her eyes issuing a challenge.

'I wondered how long you'd be. You didn't show up last night, but I knew you wouldn't stay away for long.'

'I had business to attend to.'

Emma nodded. Her voice was strangely hollow as she said, 'Police Chief Davis called around looking for you.'

'I'll call him back in a while. Can we go upstairs?'

Emma gave him a coy smile. 'Already?'

'Yes.'

Emma headed for the hallway. Slim glanced back at the glass on the worktop, then scooped it up and slammed the drink back as he followed Emma into the hall. Emma was waiting at the foot of the stairs. Slim slipped past her and headed up to the second floor. Instead of going to Emma's room, he went into Ted's.

Emma followed him as far as the doorway, then stopped. 'So soon? Don't you want one last time with me?'

Slim ignored her. He walked around the bed and drew back the drapes. In the driveway, Arthur's patrol car sat alongside Emma's car.

Slim sighed, then turned to the bed and picked up the little teddy bear he had given Emma to put in Ted's hotel room.

'When did you kill her?' he said.

Emma looked at him. She frowned, cocked her head, then gave a little illegible mumble. After a second attempt at finding a voice, she muttered, 'I like you, Slim. Don't you like me?'

'I'd like to say I've met worse people, but I'm not sure that I have.'

'For a man like you to judge me—'

'I've never killed a child.'

Emma looked down. Her voice trembled as she said, 'I only meant to scare her.'

'Was it harder to live with Becca or with Joanna?'

Emma shook her head, rolling her eyes as the same time as though trying to brush off a fly. 'I must say, it took

The Man by the Sea

you a long time to figure it all out. I imagine there are worse detectives in the world, but there can't be many.'

'I'm something of a novice.'

Even as he spoke, Slim felt a tingle running down his legs. It felt like the first drink for a while, only much stronger.

'Goddamn it, What was in that drink?'

Emma smiled. 'Something the hospital gave me.' She shrugged. 'To help me sleep.'

'How did you know I'd drink it?'

'You're an addict. Of course you would.' She lifted her hand, and something glinted between her fingers: a razor blade. 'Though my confidence isn't what it was. I'm glad I didn't have to use this. I really do like you, Slim. In another time, another place ... maybe.'

Slim's legs buckled. Emma came forward as his knees hit the floor. He tried to lift his hands to defend himself, but his arms were as useless as two logs taped to the sides of his body.

He felt her pushing him back, rolling him onto his front, then the blur that his vision had become faded to nothing.

58

The entirety of Slim's body felt as though it had been twisted around and replaced back to front. He opened his eyes as a breeze ruffled his hair.

'Huh?'

The Lancashire coast laid itself out before him in a series of inlets and jagged headlands. Slim recognised the curve of Cramer Cove to his left. A stormy November tide battered the foreshore.

'Are you wondering how you got up here?'

Slim turned to find Emma sitting beside him, cross legged, looking out to sea. She was wearing a parka jacket, the hood pulled up, framing her hair around her face. As she glanced at him, Slim caught shades of long-forgotten actresses in the cut of her jaw, a reminder of what might have been.

'There's another road,' she continued. 'It goes up to the headland. We borrowed Chief Davis's patrol car, which can handle roads like that a lot better than my little thing. I had to push you out along the path, though.'

'Push me?'

The Man by the Sea

'Ted woke up yesterday. It appears from new hospital reports that he might be paralyzed, but the doctors aren't sure yet. They gave me the chair to figure out the house. What I'd need to move about, where I'd need to put in ramps, that kind of thing. It wasn't easy, though. The coastal path isn't exactly designed for it. Thank god it hadn't rained.' She smiled. 'I'd have had to drag you.'

'You're strong.'

She shrugged again. 'I guess it's all the climbing. I had a lot of time for hobbies, What with Ted always at work or on his pretend business trips.'

'I can't believe it took me so long to see it. The hints were there, weren't they? You were playing me for a fool all along.'

Emma sighed. 'You weren't supposed to get so involved. I wanted to know what he was doing, whether he was still looking for her. That was all. I didn't want all those dark days dredged up again. You don't get it, do you? I loved him.'

'I should have twigged you were following me when you showed up at my house,' Slim said. 'I never told you where I lived. And when my recording equipment switched itself on.'

'Joanna ... I miss you,' Emma said in a male voice that sent a shiver racing down Slim's spine. Emma grinned. 'It's some way off, isn't it? But it was enough to fool you. You just needed to hear a man's voice to be convinced.'

'You called him Ted. Joanna called him Eddie, didn't she? I missed that, too.'

'You'd never make a cop, Slim.'

'And that box you gave me, you knew it had nothing of any use to me.'

'I missed a couple of things. That's why I had Joanna burn it.'

'Were you trying to kill me?'

Emma nodded. 'I panicked. When I realised you'd gone out, I had to play the thankful lover.' She frowned, her lip trembling as though she might cry. 'I was thankful, though. Isn't that strange? I'm not joking, Slim. You've come to mean as much as anyone.'

'But not as much as Ted?'

'No one could ever mean as much as Ted. He was my world. As she was his. That's why, Slim. That's why everything.'

Slm tried to reach into his pocket, but for the first time realised his hands were bound behind his back with electrical ties.

'The flyer is in my pocket,' Slim said.

Emma reached over and pulled out the faded picture of the theatre group. She smiled fondly and pointed at a girl near the end of the line.

'There I am.'

'I didn't recognise you at first, but you were there all along.'

Emma sniffed. 'Don't feel bad. Ted didn't recognise me either. When I met him again in eighty-nine, he thought we were strangers. He didn't care much about my past, so I just changed my home town and my school, and he thought nothing of it. I called myself Emmie Clovelly back then. I actually did better than either of them, with a couple of minor television parts in the mid-Eighties. I was never her, though. I was never Juliet.'

'You killed Joanna out of jealousy.'

'When I found him again, I thought my world had exploded. Everything I had ever wanted, Ted was it. I

The Man by the Sea

didn't care where we went, what we did, I just wanted his arms around me, his eyes on my face. At first I thought our romance was real, that he truly loved me, and I wanted it so much that I just went along with it. I deluded myself for a while, but eventually I realised he was looking through me, seeing someone else. Seeing her.'

'How did you know?'

Emma laughed. 'A woman always knows. Ted was as open as a summer market. Ted, he wrote everything down.'

'I found his diary.'

Emma nodded. 'A lucky spot. I left that there after I noticed you'd found it. I wondered what you'd think. One of the reasons I hired you was because he'd stopped writing in it. I fought tooth and nail over moving back to Carnwell, because I knew he couldn't give up on her, he couldn't give up on the myth. In the end it was out of my hands. His company transferred him. I thought he'd finally given up on her after the old lady died, but then I found out about his missing Fridays.'

'But Joanna was long dead by then, of course?'

Emma let out a long breath. 'Around 'Ninety-one, I think. I knew Ted thought he'd seen her, and there were rumours about a woman haunting Cramer Cove. I came with him on a business trip and while he was in a meeting I drove down to the beach, and there I found her.'

'At Cramer Cove.'

'She was sitting by the water's edge. She looked a mess. When I talked to her, I realised there was little left of the girl I had idolised. She could barely speak, and what she did say made little sense. Too much exposure to water and salty air had ruined her skin, and her clothes were rags on rags. She was homeless, stealing from bins around

Carnwell, scavenging what she could for her secret little lair. She was there in plain view. No one notices the homeless, do they?'

'You followed her to the cave?'

Emma scoffed. 'She showed me. Oh yeah, Joanna Bramwell knew Emmie Clovelly all right. Unlike Ted, she noticed me right away. I think she thought we were friends.'

'But you killed her?'

Emma shivered as though caught by a sudden gust of wind. 'I hit her with a rock when her back was turned. She had picked up this flyer, pointed at me to prove she knew me. After that I saw red. I left her there. After all, where else could I hide her where I knew she'd never be found?'

'And you put the bookmark back in the book?'

'It was lying open. She had been reading it in the light of the borehole.'

Slim felt another shiver. He thought about telling Emma what he had learned about the last hours Ted and Joanna were together, but now, at the end of everything, it made no difference.

'Ted suffered, too,' was all he could think to say.

'We all suffered,' Emma said. 'We just dealt with it in different ways.'

'I can see that.'

Emma turned to him, tears in her eyes. 'Can you, really? I spent my life competing against a ghost. All I wanted was Ted. You think I'm a monster? I've had one on my back my whole life. Her name is Joanna Bramwell.'

'He destroyed your life, so you destroyed his, by turning Joanna Bramwell into an object of fear, and using her memory to haunt him. You killed those three women to get back at him.'

The Man by the Sea

Emma shook her head. 'I killed none of them. Becca ... I never meant to hurt her, and Elizabeth ... I only meant to scare her. Andrea, though, that was before my time.'

'She fell from the rocks.'

'I read about it. I think Joanna tried to talk to her, and scared her into attempting an impossible climb. If you didn't know Joanna ... if you weren't looking for her ... she was fearsome.'

'But I found those piles of stones you left. There were more near Ted's crash.'

Emma smiled. 'So you do notice some things? It was a game. I saw a photo of Andrea's body once. I saw the stones, guessed Joanna had tried to cover the body, in her simple way.'

'Like a mourner?'

'Yes. I remembered it after Becca died. I panicked, and to the sharp-eyed it tied the two deaths together. I had no alibi for Becca, but for Andrea I was living in Manchester. I was safe.'

'And with Elizabeth it became a game again?'

Emma shrugged. 'Why not? I'd got away with it once.'

Slim sighed. 'How did you deal with it? How did you deal with the guilt?'

Emma shook her head. 'I'm not sure if I did. I put it away, and tried to forget, and when it reared its head, I did it over again. Isn't that how anyone deals with something traumatic? You have to, don't you? Otherwise it would drive you mad.'

Boots in the sand.

Slim nodded. 'I think I understand you. I could never forgive what you did, but on a certain level I understand why you did it.'

Emma gave a sad laugh. 'You're a useless detective, but you'd have made a great counsellor.'

'I guess I never found my true path either. So what happens now? You know you'll never get away with it. You'll be caught if you run.'

'I know that, of course.' Emma sighed. 'Look, it's almost sunset. It's a good time, don't you think? It fits with the theme and everything.'

Emma stood up and took a few steps forward, craning her neck to peer down at the rocks. Slim suddenly understood what she meant to do. He began straining at his bonds, but he was tied too tight.

'Emma, no ... you don't have to do this. We can figure something out. I don't want to—'

She looked back, and gave him a smile that for a moment was filled with all the radiance of a beauty hidden behind years of pain. 'Whether you live or die is up to you, Slim. It's not my choice to decide what you do with your life.'

'Emma ... what?'

'You think I'd kill you, the one person who made me feel like her?' She sniffed. 'I was Juliet for a while, wasn't I?'

'Emma?'

'You'll figure something out. You were military after all. They must have taught you about these things.'

She turned and walked away toward the cliff edge.

'Emma, no!'

'Goodbye, Slim. I hope I won't be remembered ... like her.'

Slim struggled, wanting to follow, but the bonds on his legs wouldn't let him get up. As the sun dipped, Emma became a silhouette, and then she was gone.

59

A PAIR OF DOG WALKERS FOUND A TRUSSED AND struggling Slim halfway down the path to the beach. With temperatures rapidly dropping, they helped cut him free and get him to safety.

By the time he had made his way back to Carnwell Police Station, Arthur's body had been discovered. While information was difficult to obtain, Slim was able to ascertain that the police chief had been found in the Douglas's dining room, killed by a blow to the back of the head with a blunt object, most likely an ornamental vase found nearby.

Slim, with his fingerprints all over the Douglas's house, was considered a suspect, and knew he would spend many hours in police interview rooms, but because he was not considered a threat, he was released, provided he stayed in the area while the investigation was ongoing.

A week later, he received a call to inform him that he was no longer under suspicion and was free to do as he pleased, provided he remained available for contact in the event that he was required to provide evidence.

Despite search teams working twenty-four hours a day, Emma's body remained unrecovered. Slim could only hope that she had found peace at last, and while in a confusing way he pined for her despite what she had done, in many ways he was glad to have brought the case to a conclusion, even if there were threads that might never be fully resolved.

'Arthur's last message to me, it was to say that the photographs I took on the clifftop showed Emma,' he told the man sitting across from him in the cafe on Carnwell's high street. His hands shook slightly as he held the coffee cup—three days sober and it was better as the hours passed. 'I went up to the fishing cabin and it was still there, the costume she wore, hidden in the roof space.'

'What did you do with it?'

'Nothing. It's still there.'

Ted Douglas nodded. 'Could you do me a favour, Mr Hardy? Could you burn it, please?'

Slim looked into the eyes across the table from his, and saw weariness beyond even that he saw in his own.

'If that's what you want.'

Ted nodded. 'It is. Thank you.'

He made to stand up, reaching for a pair of crutches resting against the edge of the table.

'Can I help you with that?'

Ted shook his head. 'I'll manage,' he said. 'That's about all I can do now, isn't it?'

'I wish there was something I could say.'

Ted shook his head. 'I don't think there is.' As he steadied himself with one hand, he reached out to shake Slim's hand with the other.

'Good luck with everything, Mr Hardy. I can't imagine this has been easy on you, either.'

Slim opened his mouth to respond, but could think of nothing to say. Instead he gave a short nod, then watched as Ted limped away to the door, out into the street beyond, and away into the world.

#####

ABOUT THE AUTHOR

Jack Benton is a pen name of Chris Ward, the author of the dystopian *Tube Riders* series, the horror/science fiction *Tales of Crow* series, and the *Endinfinium* YA fantasy series, as well as numerous other well-received stand alone novels.

The Man by the Sea is his first attempt at writing a mystery.

Chris would love to hear from you:
www.amillionmilesfromanywhere.net
chrisward@amillionmilesfromanywhere.net

ACKNOWLEDGMENTS

This book was something of a departure for me. It was my first attempt to write a mystery, and was written in a way I've never tried before—entirely on a smartphone. I think it turned out rather well, and I hope that you, the reader, will agree.

Special thanks to Melanie Earnshaw for your insights into all things to do with law enforcement, and to Jenny Twist for your notes and encouragement.

And finally, thank you to my readers. You make all the lonely hours of writing worth it.

Printed in Great Britain
by Amazon